RAAVI PAAR AND OTHER STORIES

Gulzar was born in Deena (Pakistan) in 1934. He was brought up in Delhi and later moved to Bombay.

In the film world, he has worked with Bimal Roy, Hrishikesh Mukherjee, Hemant Kumar and others. During his long and celebrated career, Gulzar has written many melodious and meaningful songs. He started writing screenplays and scripts, which were like a breath of fresh air in the film industry. Later he got into direction and made the most poignant and significant films.

Gulzar has written the scripts for now nearly fifty films and has directed several, some of which are *Mere Apne, Aandhi, Mausam, Khushboo, Kinara, Meera, Parichay, Lekin, Libaas* and, most recently in 1997, *Maachis,* for which he received national and international acclaim and several awards. Gulzar has also made two serials for television: *Kirdar* and *Mirza Ghalib.*

By the same Author

SILENCES
Translated by Rina Singh

PUKHRAJ

CHAND PUKHRAJ KA

RAAT PASHMINE KI (Hindi)

RAAVI PAAR (Hindi)

MIRZA GHALIB (English, Hindi, Urdu)

RAAVI PAAR
AND OTHER STORIES

Gulzar

RUPA

Published by
Rupa Publications India Pvt. Ltd 1997, 2006
7/16, Ansari Road, Daryaganj
New Delhi 110002

Sales centres:
Allahabad Bengaluru Chennai
Hyderabad Jaipur Kathmandu
Kolkata Mumbai

First published in hardcover in 1997.

This is a work of fiction. Names, characters, places and
incidents are either the product of the author's imagination or
are used fictitiously, and any resemblance to any actual persons,
living or dead, events or locales is entirely coincidental.

ISBN: 978-81-291-1013-8

Seventh impression 2017

10 9 8 7

The moral right of the author has been asserted.

Typeset by Mindways Design, New Delhi

For Raakhee
the longest short story of my life

contents

foreword

Writing a short story is an experience of thought to me. It is something more than a sheer feeling. It needs a little more narrative than a poem. My stories are as short as they can be, except perhaps for *Junglenama, Habu Tames Fire* and *Seema*. I required to elaborate at length, the covert thought present in them, to share the experience with my readers.

Some of my stories are biographical, which like biographical novels, are not oft trod territory. I have tried to write, for the first time, a short story in the same genre, highlighting a major incident in the lives of those persons. *Bimalda* and *Michelangelo* are two of them. The latter's incident is like a parable, which I found extremely profound in its interpretation. The story is like the legendary Baiju Bawra-Tansen confrontation, which finds no witness in our history. It has no written record, but the parable or the legend lives on. There are many such more in our history.

I am fond of travelling in time and space. In due course of 'time', I may come up with some more stories, which in a sense 'travel'. I undertook a similar journey to look at the extinguished star, Eta Coriniae's impression on one part of our Mother – Earth. It becomes all the more relevant now, since the graves of the star poets of all times, Zauq and Ghalib have been discovered recently in very shabby conditions in Delhi. Ghalib's grave was rotting for a number of years! Zauq's was discovered under a public lavatory! (I hope it makes sense the way I reacted on the situation.)

I had witnessed the partition of India from very close quarters in 1947. It left me bruised and scarred. I cannot help, but write about that excruciating period. I wrote the stories with the background of the partition to try and get the painful experience out of my system. On sharing them with my readers, I hope very much to distance myself from the stories. My only wish, that these stories do not re-ignite the latent fear and anguish, once again, in some readers who witnessed the gory partition with their own eyes.

Some of these stories were written long, long back, like *Jamun ka Per*, and *Kagaz ki Topi*. I was not sure whether to include them or not, but Sanjana was keen. So here they are. My sincere thanks to Meghna who went through the manuscript so carefully and to Deena for putting them into the perfect chronological order.

This venture would have remained just a dream if not for the commendable effort of Masooma Ali who has painstakingly translated my stories from Hindi and Urdu. I would also like to thank Alok Bhalla for his contribution. I hope this endeavour of ours finds favour with the readers.

16.5.97

khauf

His nerves were on edge with fear. As he sat his knees shook so much it seemed as if he was about to have an epileptic fit.

There had been riots in the city for the last four days. The curfew was lifted for a few hours in the morning and in the evening. During those hours some people went out quickly to buy a few essential things for the day, while others went out quickly to create trouble — to set fire, stab, or leave a few corpses behind — and went back home even before the curfew was reimposed. Bombay was overflowing with hot news and hot blood, even though the radio and T.V. continuously announced that the situation in the city was under control and that life was returning to normal.

In order to prove that the situation was normal, local trains had begun to run again since the previous day. Even though most of the compartments were empty, the sight of lights on the railway tracks helped to somewhat dispel the darkness of the last few days. The sound of a train rattling past the settlements on both sides of the tracks, over which a heavy and stony silence had settled, brought back hope of life again.

Yasin used to listen to the rattle and also often got up to watch the trains pass by. Tomorrow would be the fifth day of his absence from home. They must have given up waiting for me, he thought. Must have begun to search for me. The day was about to come to an end when his patience snapped. As soon as the curfew was lifted in the evening, he went to Andheri station. The platform was deserted, but the indicator was still flashing the schedule of the trains.

The train pulled into the platform slowly, unlike its usual style — as if it was scared, afraid, cautious. There were a few passengers on the train. He couldn't decide which compartment he should enter. The majority of the passengers were Hindus, gathered together in groups of twos and fours. He continued to hesitate on the platform, but jumped into a compartment the moment the train started. He chose an empty compartment. He looked all around carefully and then sat huddled in the corner seat of the last berth from where he could keep an eye on the entire compartment. He began to breathe more easily as the train picked up speed.

Suddenly, Yasin saw a shape emerge from the other end of the compartment. He nearly fainted. His knees began to tremble again. He crouched so that if the man came towards him, he could either hide under the berth, or confront him — take up position in front of him.

The door of the compartment wasn't far. If he jumped out of the running train, he faced no other danger except death. Even if the train slowed down, then the man ... Suddenly, the man stood up in his place. He stood and looked all around. There was no sign of fear or nervousness on his face. He was most certainly a Hindu — that was Yasin's first reaction. The man slowly walked up to the door at the other end of the compartment and stood near it. His muffler fluttered in the breeze like a torn flag. He continued to look outside for some time. Then it seemed as if the man was testing his strength against something. Yasin couldn't see him clearly from where he was sitting. It seemed, however, that the man was either pulling something, pushing against it or trying to lift it. Yasin thought that he was breaking something. Suddenly, the rusty door moved with a jerk and banged shut with a loud rattle. It was lucky that Yasin didn't let out a scream. Even the man was startled and looked all around him. He looked for a long time in the direction where Yasin was hiding. Yasin suspected that the man had either seen or heard him. The man's strength had added to his fear. If there was a confrontation would he be able to fight him? ... The man slowly walked towards the door on the opposite side and stood near it.

The train crossed a deserted station in Jogeshwari. If it had stopped, Yasin would have got off. But the area was under curfew and the train did not stop there ... Perhaps, the curfew bound areas would have been safer — at least the police would have been around. Now even the army had been called out to patrol the city. One could see army trucks, with green and khaki stripes, roaming through riot-torn areas, loaded with armed soldiers in green and khaki uniforms, their rifles ready, pointing out of the trucks. The police had become quite useless. No one was even afraid of it. Mobs threw stones and soda-water bottles at policemen fearlessly — and even bulbs filled with acid. When the police fired tear-gas shells, people in the mob picked them up with wet handkerchiefs and threw them back at the police. What action had the police taken when the bakery in Sakinaka, where he worked, had been set on fire? The police had stood at a distance and watched the spectacle, while they themselves had to run through narrow lanes to save their lives and hide in a garage of battered and half-stripped cars. There had been eight to ten of them. God bless Bhau! As they were running, Bhau had grabbed him by his shirt and pulled him into a small shed next to a tea-shop. Bhau knew that he was a Muslim. Bhau was a Hindu. Why had he run? Bhau had told him that a blood-thirsty mob never stopped to find out the names of its victims. Its thirst was either quenched by blood or by fire. Burn it. Kill him. Destroy everything. Its anger cools down only when nothing remained before it.

The rattling of the other door startled him. That man had now shut both the doors at the other end of the compartment. He stared for sometime in the direction where Yasin was hiding. Fear gripped him once again. Why was that man shutting the doors of the compartment? Did he want to kill him, and, leaving his blood-soaked corpse on the train, get off at the next station? The train was slowing down — it was approaching a station. The man's steps were more confident than before. He was slowly walking towards Yasin. Yasin's breathing grew more laboured. He felt cold sweat trickle down his face out of sheer terror. His breathing became heavy.

He couldn't swallow his saliva. If only he wouldn't start hiccupping, or coughing, otherwise, lying under the berth, he would be ....

The train stopped at a station. The man calmly walked upto the door which opened onto the platform and stood next to it. He had one hand in his pocket. He must have a weapon in it — a pistol, a knife? Yasin thought of making a dash for it and jumping out of the other end. But by the time he got out of his hiding place, that man would have ripped open his stomach. Why only his stomach? His throat too, so that he couldn't scream. He peeped out like a thief. That man was looking out of the train. The platform was utterly desolate — one couldn't even hear footsteps. Yasin wanted someone to come into the compartment. But how did he know who would come in? A Hindu? A Muslim? Let it be another Hindu. He may be kind-hearted like Bhau. How readily had Bhau made him wear his sacred thread and escorted him from the tea-shop upto his own small room. He had kept Yasin there for four days.

Bhau had told him, "I am a Maratha, but I don't eat meat everyday. If you want, I'll get some for you. I am not sure what kind would be available. I don't understand anything about *halal-walal*. The situation outside is so bad that vegetables are rotting in Andheri but there is no one to sell them. You can loot as much as you want."

The radio, however, continuously announced "The situation in the city is slowly returning to normal. The trains are running. In some areas, even the buses have begun to ply again."

During those four days, he had been very worried about

his family. Even they must have been worried about him. He was afraid of one thing though, Fatima going to the bakery to look for him. He could see the railway tracks from the hovel he was hiding in. He could also see the trains but Bhau had not let him go.

The train started with a jerk and brought Yasin back to the present with a jolt. That man was holding the door-handle with his left hand and standing complacently. His right hand was still in his pocket. The train crawled and dragged itself for some distance. Why didn't it pick up speed? There could be no reason for not getting the signal, not many trains were plying anyway — no train had yet gone in the opposite direction. The train continued to drag itself slowly for a long time. It continued to crawl and, finally, it stopped on the Bhayander Bridge. Below it was the bay from which, according to newspaper reports, dead bodies were often fished out.

Yasin found it difficult to breathe. Terror had made life impossible. Why doesn't that man take his hand out of his pocket? It was obvious from the look in his eyes that he was about to attack. What would happen when he attacked? Would he ask him to come out? Or would he grab him by his hair, pull him out and, in a flash, place a knife at his throat? What would he do? Why doesn't he do something?

Suddenly, the man pulled his hand out of his pocket and began to pull and push against the door again, to shut the third door. Now all the routes of escape were being closed. In any case, there was the sea down below. He would certainly be killed if he jumped. He had reached the extreme edge of fear: he was being trapped in a cave.

He suddenly jumped up from his hiding place. That man

looked at him with shocked surprise. He put his hand in his pocket. Yasin didn't know where he got the strength from. He shouted, "Ya Ali," grabbed the man's legs and threw him out. As the man fell, Yasin heard him scream, "Allah ... "

Yasin stood still. The train began to move. Yasin was surprised — "Was he also a Muslim?" But having freed himself from the noose of terror, he felt as if he had escaped from the jaws of death.

That night he told Fatima, "It had to happen that way. I had no immediate proof of being a Muslim myself."

sunset boulevard

Even during the post-mortem, Mishraji's visiting card lay in the fist of the corpse.

As usual, Charuji got up at five-thirty that morning. But she was a little more excited than she normally was. She was always well-dressed when she went out for her walk. Her hair was combed, she rubbed her face lightly with cream so as to disguise the wrinkles which had begun to appear on it with age. Her clothes were proof of her good taste and style.

She always told Shivdutt, "See, even today people whisper when they see me and tell each other that I am Charulataji. If not for myself, I should at least live in style for my admirers."

Shivdutt was her cook. When he saw her, she was standing before a mirror and talking to herself. She blushed coyly. Shivdutt smiled. Even at that age Madam hadn't given up the habit of blushing. It was the smile which had conquered many a heart when she was young.

"Shivdutt, someone called Gopal Das Mishra is coming to see me. Make some tea for him."

"Who is he?" Shivdutt asked, a little surprised.

"A writer. He wants to write a book about me."

That was the reason for the extra bounce in her walk! It was many years after her retirement from the film industry that someone had remembered that lonely soul. In the beginning many journalists used to call on her. But how could people call on her everyday at her house situated far away in Mahabaleshwar? Charulata, however, continued to hope that the tide would soon turn in her favour. After sometime, the number of visitors dwindled. She was offered a few roles suitable for her age, but she refused to play the roles of old women. She often stood before her mirror with her head tilted backwards and looked at herself. There were no creases on her neck: no signs of old age, she argued with herself. The reflection in the mirror, however, didn't tell her, "You are getting old." Those words are spoken by reflections only in films.

Of course, after her first spot of heart trouble, Dr. Sahni had told her, "Listen, your heart can no longer take the stress you make it undergo. One day, it'll blow it's fuse."

Shivdutt informed her that Mishraji had arrived.

"What? Yes — Mishraji," Charulata was startled to hear the name even though she had been waiting for him.

"Ask him to sit down in the hall below. Did you remove the coverings from the sofas?"

"Yes, Madam."

"And the chandeliers? Have you lit them?"

"Yes, Madam."

Shivdutt knew his duties well. He still used to boast about Madam to everyone. If, once in a while, she received a letter from an admirer, he would talk about it at ten different places in the market.

As she was putting on her necklace, Charulata felt that her neck had become a little thin. If only she still had her broad necklace! It would have covered her neck. But she had sold it two years ago. She had bought it a long time ago for three thousand rupees and had sold it for thirty thousand! If Singh Sahib had been alive, he wouldn't have let her sell it.

As Charulata came down the stairs, she looked just like a film star. She imagined that a voice would soon call out, "Start sound, Camera!"

Mishraji was carefully examining the marble statues in the hall. He was carrying a pad in his hand. He had perhaps made a few notes on it.

When he saw Charuji, he folded his hands and greeted her with great courtesy.

"Please, sit down."

Mishraji sat down on the sofa. Charuji's personality could still charm people. Mishraji found himself unable to say anything for sometime. It was lucky that Shivdutt came in with the tea-tray. He also brought some sweets and some savoury snacks on two separate plates.

Charuji poured out the tea.

"How did you find my address?"

"Goel Sahib gave it to me. Isn't he your manager in

Bombay?"

"Yes. Goel is a very fine person. He managed my affairs for many years. Even now he looks after some of my work. Please have some tea."

"And, then, time just passed me by," Charuji continued to talk. "I love to be left alone and in peace. I have never liked to work hard. Even in the past, I never acted in too many films, though there was a crowd of producers who beseiged me day and night. Finally, I ran away and came here to hide."

"May I look around your house?"

"Yes, why not? Please come."

Charuji led him upto the marble statues.

"We brought this pair back from Italy. It was difficult to bring them across undamaged. For many years, they were placed in my house in Bombay. You, perhaps, never visited that house?"

"No," he answered dryly, but he had a broad smile on his face.

As they walked through the corridor, Charuji told him, "We built this house with great love and care. Singh Sahib and I used to have lots of fights over it. Sometimes about the bricks to be used, sometimes over the kind of wood to be bought. Singh Sahib brought those tiles from Bangalore. I chose the name of the house from an English film — *Sunset Boulevard*. And ... and this cage ... we never kept a bird in it. I don't know where he got it from. One day ..." she began to laugh loudly. It seemed as if she was performing a scene. Even Shivdutt looked in. He had never seen Madam laugh like that before. Yes, there was a time when she used to do so — when Noor and Neela visited her. Heroines who were her contemporaries.

Charuji said, as she led him up the stairs, "I told him, why don't you imprison me in that cage. He replied, 'I'll have to build it in marble.' I love marble very much. I like walking on it with my bare-feet. Singh Sahib ... that's his portrait ..."

It was Singh Sahib's life-size portrait. It hung on the upper verandah. There were candle-stands on either side of it. Shivdutt had lit the candles in them. He knew that she would pass that way.

She continued to gaze at Singh Sahib's face in silence for sometime. Then she wiped both her eyes, bowed her head and turned away. Mishraji walked behind her. She said, "Our married life was very brief. Only three years, four months and eighteen days."

She sobbed once more. Shivdutt had by then removed the tray from the hall. Charuji called out to him to fetch some water. When he didn't reply, she realized that he was outside on the lawn. She found the silence uncomfortable.

She turned around and said to Mishraji, "Is there anything you'd like to ask me in particular?"

"What would be the area of this house?"

She looked at him with surprise, "Area?"

"And the built up area?"

Charuji seemed to shrivel up. She said slowly, "Goel should know."

"Never mind, I'll find out from Goel Sahib," Mishraji stood up.

Charuji stood, leaning with her full weight against the arms of the sofa.

"Why did Goel send you here?"

"To look at this house. It may be up for sale soon. He asked me to evaluate it and find a customer who would be willing ..."

"What's your name?" Charulata asked sharply.

"Dheeraj Mishra. Property Broker. I buy and sell property." He gave her his card.

Suddenly, her face turned red. She wanted to scream, but controlled herself. No sound escaped from her mouth. With a sweep of her hand, she asked him to leave.

The broker tried to justify himself, "Goel Sahib had asked me not to talk to you. He had said that you would perhaps ..."

"Get out," Charulata screamed this time. But her voice cracked a little.

The broker got nervous and left at once.

With his card clutched in her hand, she watched him till he left. As she turned around and started climbing the stairs, she staggered. She had a heart-attack and ...

She was still clutching the visiting card in her fist at the time of the post-mortem.

dhuan

Starting in rather an innocuous manner, the smoke neverthe-less engulfed the entire *qasbah* in no time at all.

Chaudhary had passed away at four in the morning. After crying desperately till seven, Chaudhrine collected her wits about her. The first person she sent for was Mullah Khairuddin. The servant was warned strictly not to mention anything to him. After the servant showed the Mullah into the courtyard and left, Chaudhrine led him to the bedroom upstairs where Chaudhary's dead body had been placed on the floor. You could see a fair but pallid face with white eyebrows and a beard and long hair to match between two white sheets. The face looked extremely serene.

The Mullah promptly pronounced '*Innalillah-e-wa-in-a-Allehe-Rajeoon*' and uttered a few conventional words of condolence. Before he could seat himself properly, Chaudhrine took out her husband's will from the almirah and gave it to him to read. According to the testament, Chaudhary's last wish was to be cremated and not buried after his death. Further, he wished that his ashes be mingled with the water of the river which irrigated his land.

The Mullah fell silent after reading the will. He was aware of Chaudhary's contribution towards the spiritual life of his village. He used to give generous donations to both Hindus and Muslims. With his help the mud structure of the mosque had been converted in to a *pucca* building. He had also developed the Hindu cremation ground with bricks and mortar. Chaudhary had been unwell for four years but all through his illness, arrangements for the 'iftari' of the poor were made by him in the mosque every year all through the month of Ramazan. The Muslims of the area had great faith in him. The Mullah was astonished to read his will. He became apprehensive that it may create a rumpus. As it was, the atmosphere in the country had been vitiated of late. Hindus had become more Hindu and Muslims more Muslim.

Chaudhrine said, "I do not want any rituals. All I want is for you to arrange to cremate him at the *shamshan*. I could have told Ramchandra Pandit but I did not send for him because I do not want anything going wrong."

However, things did go wrong when Mullah Khairuddin summoned Pandit Ram Chandra and advised him, "Please do not give permission to cremate Chaudhary in your *shamshan*. It can lead to a turmoil amongst the Muslims of the area. Chaudhary was not an ordinary man after all. A whole lot of people are associated with him in many ways."

Pandit Ram Chandra assured him that he did not want any mischief in their area. Before the word gets to the people, he would explain things to relevant persons.

The spark that had been ignited, slowly started to blaze forth in flames.

"It is not a question involving Chaudhary or Chaudhrine, it is a question of faith. It is a question involving the entire community and religion. How dare did the Chaudhrine agree to cremate rather than bury Chaudhary? Isn't she familiar with the tenets of Islam?"

Some people insisted on meeting Chaudhrine. She explained to them patiently, "Brothers, it was his last wish. A corpse is either buried or cremated. Why should you object if his soul finds peace through cremation?"

One gentleman reacted sharply, "Do you think you'll be at peace with yourself after burning him?"

"Yes," she answered briefly, "I'll be at peace with myself after carrying out his last wish."

She grew restless as the day advanced. What she wanted to accomplish through peaceful negotiations began to be blown out of all proportions. There was no complex intrigue or mystery behind Chaudhary Saheb's last wish. Nor did it connect to any philosophy relating to religious faith or conviction. It was just a simple, human desire to obliterate all signs of his earthly existence after his death.

"I am when I am, I don't exist when I don't."

He had said that to his wife several years ago but such things are not taken seriously while one is still alive. He had stated the same thing in his will. Carrying out his last wish was the proof of his confidence in the love and fidelity of his wife. You could not possibly forget all your commitments the moment someone is out of sight.

Chaudhrine sent Biru to call Pandit Ram Chandra to her house but he was not available. His colleague said, "Look, we'll definitely chant the *mantras* and apply *tilak* before cremating Chaudhary."

"I say, how can you convert a man to another religion after his death?" Biru protested.

"Please don't argue. It is not possible to administer 'mukhagni' without reciting 'mantras' from the holy *Geeta*. If we do it, the soul of the deceased would not find deliverance. And such a restless soul would then torment all of us. We are indebted to Chaudhary Saheb for so many things. We can't possibly let his soul down."

Biru went back.

Panna had seen Biru leaving the Pandit's house. He went and informed the people in the mosque.

Flames leapt up suddenly from the fire which was about to go cold after smouldering for some time. Four or five reliable Muslims went to the extent of passing their verdict. They were obliged to Chaudhary Saheb for a lot and they were not going to let his soul wander around without a burial. Collectively, they sent orders for digging a grave in the cemetery at the rear of the mosque.

By evening a few people landed up at the *haveli* again. They were determined to put pressure on Chaudhrine to part with the document of the will so that it could be destroyed. What could the old crone do when there was no evidence of the will?

Chaudhrine seemed to have sensed their strategy. She concealed the will and when people tried to threaten her, she said, "Ask Mullah Khairuddin. He has seen and read the will."

"Supposing he denies it?"

"If he denies having read it with his hand placed on the *Quran*, I'll show it, otherwise ...."

"Otherwise what?"

"Otherwise you can see it in the court."

It became clear that the matter could be taken to the court. It was likely that Chaudhrine might call her lawyer and the police from the city. She could go ahead with her intention to cremate her husband in the presence of the police. Who knows, she may have already sent for them. Otherwise how could anyone talk with such self-possession while her husband's corpse was resting on slabs of ice?

Rumours spread like fire at night. Someone said, "A man riding a horse has just been seen going in the direction of the city. The rider had muffled his head and face under a turban and he was coming from the direction of Chaudhary's *haveli*."

One person said he had seen the rider emerging from Chaudhary's stable.

Khadu stated that he had not only heard the sound of wood being chopped in the backyard of the *haveli*, but also seen a tree being felled.

Chaudhrine was definitely making arrangements to set up a pyre in the backyard. Kalloo's blood began to boil.

"Cowards! A Muslim is going to be burned on a pyre tonight. Would you all sit here and watch the flames?

Kalloo came out of his *adda*. So what if violence was his

profession. There is something called religious faith too. "Even a mother is not as dear to one as his faith."

Taking four or five fellows with him, Kalloo scaled the rear wall and gained access into the *haveli*. The old woman was sitting alone by the dead body of her husband. Before she could even react, Kalloo's axe had fallen on her.

They lifted Chaudhary's corpse and carried it to the back of the mosque where a freshly dug grave was awaiting it.

As they were leaving, Ramze asked, "What happens when the body of the old woman is discovered in the morning?"

"Is she dead?"

"Her skull was split open. Would she survive till morning?"

Kalloo stopped and glanced in the direction of the old woman's bedroom. Panna understood what was in his mind.

"Carry on, Ustad. I know what you are thinking about. We'll take care of everything."

Kalloo strode away in the direction of the graveyard.

At night giant flames were leaping out of Chaudhary's bedroom and the entire *qasbah* had got engulfed in smoke.

The living were cremated and the dead, buried.

dalia

Her husband was the first to break the news, "I was summoned to the *haveli* at the behest of Maharaj today — Chhote Maharaj had sent for me — I was quite astonished."

It was her turn to be astonished now. Khuswa was telling her, his eyes wide open.

"Their servants came to the fields to get me. They tied my hands with a rope. I couldn't think of any fault or mistake I had committed. They took me away and made me stand in front of him. He looked at me with those enormous eyes lined with antimony. I was so scared. Then he ordered those two servants out and instructed them to close the door behind them. That surprised me more." Dalia felt her husband's eyes were also quite large though they have been shrunk to a smaller size by poverty and the sun. Khuswa continued,

"Then he asked me in a thunderous voice, 'Is Dalia your wife?'

Dalia was startled. She said, "Then?"

"He asked me how much I spent on drink everyday, and how much went towards household expenses. He said he had come to know that out of my daily earnings of two and half rupees I spent two rupees on drink and gave you eight annas for household expenses. I fell at his feet and said that someone had given him wrong information. I give two rupees for household expenses and spent eight annas on drink. He said he knew it all...."

Dalia understood what had happened. Just the other day she had met Maharaj in the desert. She was carrying on her head two pitchers full of water drawn from the well on the other side of the dune when his she-camel started moving in close proximity to her. She could not even look up because there were two full pitchers on her head. It seemed as if someone was speaking to her from the sky.

"Listen, girl, will you give me some water to drink?"

She had stopped short. While she was still adjusting the pitcher on her arm, Maharaj had made the she-camel sit on the sand in a folded heap.

"Will you let me drink some water? My flask has fallen empty on the way."

The enormous eyes lined with antimony had rested on her *choli*. Both her hands were holding the water vessels so she could not even pull her *pallu*.

"What happened? Why are you scared? Aren't you from Jhajure? I am the Maharaj of the palace — the Chhote Maharaj..."

She did not say a word. Maharaj did not get off the camel but kept staring at her. With trepidation she had uttered, "We are from a lower caste, *Hukum*. It would pollute the *dharma*."

"Whose dharma? Yours or mine?"

"Yours, *Hukum*."

He was silent for a moment, then laughed and before riding away said, "All right. Don't give me water. I'll drink when I reach home."

Khuswa was saying, "Maharaj told me that Raniji needed a maid in the house, someone who would attend to her bath and Neeti Tai had mentioned my wife's name. He had asked me to send you from tomorrow. You'll get clothes and food grains from the *haveli*."

Dalia shivered. Maharaj had made all the enquiries in such a short while, she wondered. Her fair skin had proved to be her enemy time and again. Her mother used to say, "Smear some dust on your face before you step out. Otherwise you would return with a blackened face someday."

And now her husband was saying. "You'll go to work in the *haveli* from tomorrow."

Dalia stood up and stamped her foot. "I'll never go to the *haveli*. Don't you know where the women who go to the *haveli* end up? They go and live in the brothels! Their men do not keep them."

Khuswa guffawed and a strong whiff of cheap liquor hit Dalia's senses. "Who is going to pay for you in a brothel? Haven't you ever seen your reflection in a mirror?"

The next day, leaving Dalia with Neeti Tai at the threshold of the *haveli*, Khuswa went off to work in the fields as usual. Neeti took her inside with many words of advice and reassurance. After crossing several doors and entrances they reached the Maharani's chambers, where she was having an oil massage. She had taken off her jewellery which lay in a huge heap on a *dhurrie*. She spoke from behind the door.

"Who is it, Tai?"

"It is Dalia. You had sent for her."

"What for?"

"To assist in your bath."

"Yes, of course. Is she neat and clean?"

Tai gave Dalia a once over and answered, "We'll wash her. She'll then be clean. She is going to be good."

Maharani's laughter tinkled like a silver rattle.

Dalia was reassured to find that her fears about the *haveli* were baseless. Nothing that she was apprehensive about took place there. The family seemed to be nice. However, she was amazed to see the interiors of the *haveli* where rooms within rooms opened up into more rooms. The *haveli* seemed to have an enormous belly which could easily contain a large number of people. Bade Maharaj spent all his time lying in an opium den in an outer room. There was Chhote Maharaj to look after the estate but he did not visit the *zenana* too often. However, you could see him in the room of Raniji sometime. Raniji used to talk a lot during her bath. She would refer to her parental home quite frequently.

"Bapu had a *stapu* made with glazed tiles for us in the courtyard. The floor used to get spoiled by the lines drawn by chalksticks so one day he sent for a mason...., do you know what tiles are? They are coloured bricks made of cement. Bapu had a *stapu* made in the courtyard where we could play hopscotch."

She stopped for a while, then asked, "What games did you play at your parent's home?"

"Where was the time for me to play, *Malkin*," Dalia answered. "I went to draw water at playtime, and worked in the field at mealtimes. My mother used to put an onion and *bajri roti* in my pocket and gave me a small piece of rock salt to lick. She instructed me to drink water before and after eating so that I would have a full stomach."

"You have started telling me how poor you were.... I was only asking what you played at as a child. All right.... will you pour water from above now?"

Tai had laughed when Dalia asked her if she could use the water with which Raniji had bathed for her own bath. She had told Dalia, "Go and bathe with fresh water, you silly girl! There is a well in the house and the wells do not run dry very often!"

The day she had brought a sliver of soap and washed with it, she would thrust her face close to Khuswa's again and again. But his nose, saturated with the stench of liquor was quite beyond smelling the perfume of the soap.

One day when she was giving a bath to Raniji they heard Maharaj calling. Raniji said to Dalia, "Go and ask him what he wants. Tell him I am bathing."

Dalia went and stood before Maharaj, "Raniji is taking her bath, *Hukum*. She has asked......"

He interrupted her, "Lift your face up. You should look at me when you talk to me." When she looked up she was stung by those enormous, antimony-lined eyes. "Tell Raniji that I am going to the lounge downstairs and to send my refreshments there."

It was the first time that she had to stand in the presence of Maharaj for so long.

He sat eating on the *jhoola* while she stood on one side holding a glass of *lassi* for him. After he finished eating he said, "Say, Dalia, you did not give me water because it would have spoiled my *dharma*. How come my *dharma* is not affected by serving me food?

"I have served you your own food, *Hukum*. There is nothing of mine in it," she answered.

"I have told you to look up while talking to me," he reminded her.

She tried hard but could not lift her eyes. She did not realize how heavy one's eyelids could be. She lifted them but they dropped back like a limp cat.

"Look up again," he demanded.

"How can I look at you like that, *Hukum*?" she said diffidently.

He took the glass of *lassi* from her hand and placing its rim under her chin, lifted her face so that she could look at him.

"Like this," he said. "Look at me and talk to me, like this. In what way do you look at that drunkard? At Khuswa?"

"But he is my husband, *Hukum*," she said defensively.

Neeti Tai came to her rescue just then. God knows how long he would have made her stand there if Tai had not come. Neeti Tai said, "Come Dalia, let me give you your food. Please let her go, *Hukum*. It is getting late."

"Hm," Maharaj snorted and asked, "do you give her enough food?"

"Malkin has told me to give her three *rotis* and a lump

of jaggery....."

Dalia drew the courage to ask, "Could I please take the *rotis* home? May I eat them at home?"

"With Khuswa?"

She nodded, "Yes."

"Tai, pack up her food and give it to her to take home. And don't count the *rotis* ... give her a whole basketful of them," Maharaj ordered.

Dalia was pleased to see Khuswa eating the butter she had brought from the *haveli*. Tai had put such a large blob of butter between the *rotis* she had brought home.

"Didn't Raniji object?" Khuswa asked.

"Well, not everything takes place in front of Raniji," she said, playfully giving one more twist to Khuswa's moustache with her butter-smeared fingers.

You could see the clouds come swirling by everyday but they just dissolved and evaporated in the sky over the desert. However, a certain current of moisture-laden breeze had pervaded the atmosphere. The earth was getting to be soft and Khuswa was much in demand as a farmhand. For the first time in years he had seen that the little granary in his house was full of foodgrains.

Dalia was rubbing oil in Raniji's hair when Maharaj entered the room without clearing his throat. He sat down before Raniji.

"Your *Mamaji*'s daughter is getting married," he said.

"Sheetla?" Raniji Asked.

"Yes, it is Sheetla's wedding and they have asked you to come early. In fact, they want you to come right now."

"You'll come too, won't you?" she asked.

"What would I do going so early? I'll be there for the wedding. You go ahead. You can stay with your parents for a few days. Ma Saheb misses you a lot," he answered.

"And who is going to look after you for so long?"

"She is here," he answered looking at Dalia, "she can take care of me. Would you, Dalia? She can stay here with Tai."

Dalia broke into a cold sweat at Maharaj's jocularity. Raniji said, "But for her husband, I would have taken her with me."

"What husband? "Maharaj said. "He is no husband. He is a bottle of liquor that rolls here and there."

Arrangements for Raniji's departure were completed in two days. A caravan left for her parent's place. Dewanji went with her as an escort.

Dalia stayed away from the *haveli* for several days after Raniji's departure. She stayed back deliberately even after Tai sent for her.

By now Khuswa was receiving somewhat higher wages from the *haveli* and his drinking had increased ever since his stocks of grain had started remaining full. Quite often, Dalia had to fetch him from the 'Theka' at night in an inebriated state.

On one occasion he picked up a fight with the village *purohit* after drinking and spat at the door of the temple in a rage. That created a furore in the village. He was beaten up by the men from the police station and put in the lock-up. Dalia visited the police station again and again. Every time she would tremble to see the state in which her husband was kept there. However, her appeals were ignored completely and ultimately she ended up going back to the *haveli*.

She became stiff sitting on the threshold of the *haveli* all day. After sunset Neeti came and took her inside. She made Dalia have a wash first and then served her something nice to eat. As she asked her to change into fresh clothes, Dalia was flabbergasted. It took her no time to understand Neeti's intent and purpose. She could read it all in Neeti's eyes.

Neeti said in a soft whisper, "Come, change your clothes. This time Khuswa is going to be kept in the lock-up for several days. And who knows what happens afterwards!"

Her voice was tremulous as she went on, "This is how I too came to Bade Maharaj and stayed back in the *haveli*. I was left with nothing with which I could go back. Maharaj did not leave me worth anything! Come, get up and change your *choli*!"

Dalia looked around with terrified eyes. Imprisoned in the belly of the *haveli*, she could hear someone bellowing close by.

faṣal

Enshrouded by the dark night, he had been hiding under the culvert for several hours. His *dhoti* was soaked in the muddy water flowing under the culvert. He had taken off his shoes and tied them to his waist and his bare feet were covered with mud. The smell of ripening corn wafting from the standing crops invigorated him. He was born of those crops. He had not brought them into existence. On the contrary, they had created him and all his fellow farmers.

"We are the ears of the corn of these crops — we are the kernel that fills the husk. But we cannot tolerate it when Thakur roasts this corn to fill his belly."

He remembered how uplifting the peasants had found his utterances. He had himself felt that he was talking like the labour leader whose speech he had heard in the city. His brother had introduced him to the leader who had told him, "You won't be able to achieve anything alone. Unless you mobilize others, the *zamindar* would chew you up like roasted corn. Let all the other farm workers join you. Get them all united and then get your land freed. *Zamindari* has long been abolished in this country."

"But how would I explain things to them? Only you can talk to them about the law."

"Let me know if I am needed and I'll come over. I'll definitely pass through your village when I go on tour."

His brother had also assured him of his support. Had their father not mortgaged his land, there would be no need for him to go to the city to become a worker in a mill.

"Once our land is restored to us, I'll come back and live in the village," his brother had said.

He had returned to the village with a lot of courage and enthusiasm. He had started talking big. He told people about forming a union and a party. Twice or thrice he was beaten up in front of other peasants. On one occasion he was even hung upside down and beaten with a wand from a tamarind tree. His wife and children implored him to give up his ways but he was like a man possessed.

His activities did not remain confined to his own village. In time he had started inciting the peasants in the neighbouring villages. He was a big hit with his audience who lapped up his speeches and responded to them with tremendous enthusiasm in his presence. However, the minute his back was turned they would revert to their usual timid selves.

It had become his style to keep a folded copy of the Hindi newspaper in his upper pocket. He had told the peasants that they were not alone in their struggle.

"A political party in the country is fighting for our rights."

As and when he felt suffocated sitting under the culvert, he would come out and let his lungs inhale their fill of the fresh air wafting over the fields.

Once he got to the town, he thought, the first thing he would do would be to contact Pandeji.

He had written a letter to Pandeji, c/o his brother, on the day he returned home after being bashed up in a neighbouring village. But no reply had come for months and when he finally heard from his brother it was just to say that Pandeji was away on tour and his letter would be delivered to him as soon as he returned. Subsequently, he had begun to hope that Pandeji would include his village in his current itenery. That had boosted his morale and he had already told the farm workers — "Be prepared. We'll have a meeting at the *chaupal* on the day Pandeji comes. You'll see what happens to that Thakur Harnam Singh then! Pandeji does not preach physical violence. He talks only of legal rights."

All the workers were aware that no one would go openly to that meeting but they saw no harm in talking about it. Such ideas, even when they were discussed in hushed tones, seemed to electrify their emaciated bodies.

However, Pandeji was delayed beyond expectation and God knows who carried tales to the Thakur. As a result he was rounded up from the fields and produced before the Thakur who, at the mention of the name of his leader, took off his double-soled shoe and struck him across the face with it.

"*Saala* Communist! Go and work in the fields, otherwise I'll have your house razed to the ground and have the land ploughed."

The threat did not in anyway end his obsession. So what if it was communism. It was acceptable to him.

On the day the Thakur's sons had abducted Loku's daughter, Loku had made frantic appeals but no one came forward to go with him to the *haveli*. But one glance at him, and he had started walking with Loku towards the *haveli*. All that the Thakur said to Loku was, "Just wait till the boys get home. I'll teach them a lesson." Then he cornered his companion and said, "How come you are taking so much interest in this affair? Are they all your offsprings? *Saale*, I'll grab your legs and split your body into two! Don't you dare to show your face to me again!!" Saying this, the Thakur gave him such a violent kick that he rolled down the stairs and fell in a heap on the ground. Loku had to carry him home on his shoulders.

The fallout of this incident was that Loku and his two sons refused to work in the fields. The battleground for rebellion was thus prepared. He was no longer alone. A party consisting of three members had already been formed.

On the third day after she was abducted, Loku's daughter committed suicide by jumping into a well. The whole village was horrified by that incident. Such incidents had shaken the village on several previous occasions too but each time they had burned themselves out like the nightly campfire at the *chaupal*. This time, however, a small crowd of about twenty people carrying burning torches assembled in front of the *haveli*. They raised slogans of *Hai, Hai* and *Harnam Singh murdabad* but the demonstration evoked absolutely no response from the *haveli*. The peasants were apprehensive that the Thakur might come to the terrace or the verandah with his rifle but nothing of the sort happened.

They had scored a point and their mood was upbeat till the next morning but when the police came to enquire into the incident, they picked up only him and took him away. He was beaten up severely but he refused to divulge any other name. All he repeated was, "The whole village was involved. Arrest them all."

He was kept in the lock-up for ten days. His fame travelled to the neighbouring villages during those ten days.

On his return to the village, he learnt that the Thakur's men had plundered and looted his house in his absence and filed a false report with the police that it was the work of the bandit Daan Singh's gang. His wife and children had found shelter in the house of Haridas from where they had sneaked out to go to his brother in the city.

His house was set ablaze at night on the same day he had arrived. He had traversed three *kos* under the cover of darkness and reached the railway station only to find that the Thakur's musclemen were stalking the place waiting for him. He escaped them by running along the *nullah* that flowed parallel to the railway track till he arrived at the culvert under which he hid himself. He knew that a goods train which passed that way after midnight slowed down as it approached the culvert.

On hearing the noise of the approaching train, he emerged from under the culvert. He had spotted the open door of a carriage from a distance and as it came close he reached out and grabbed at a bar. After dangling by it for a moment, he heaved himself up the carriage.

The moment he stepped in, he felt the muzzle of a rifle digging into his ribs.

"Who are you, *saale*? How come you have boarded this carriage?"

Another voice asked, "Are you a spy? Or a police dog?"

There was no need to ask who they were. It was common knowledge that that area was dacoit territory. However, he had now come face to face with them.

"I am a poor passenger. I am travelling without a ticket. I want to go to the city."

The bandit removed the gun and ordered him to sit in a corner. He was the lord of that carriage. His companion sat in another corner, drinking liquour off a brass tumbler.

The first outlaw returned to the door and sat down. After a brief silence he asked again, "Will you have some food? You look totally famished."

After listening to the silence for a moment, he commanded, "Move to this side. Come and sit down by *Sardar*."

Moving with some trepidation, he slid timidly towards the other side. He was too scared to stand up. *Sardar* held out a cloth bundle to him. The aroma of food wafted upto his nostrils.

"Come on, eat. There are *alu paranthas*, and pickle, too."

Sardar spoke in low, gentle tones. He opened the bundle with trembling fingers. The *paranthas* were cold but they were freshly made. After helping himself to one *parantha* he was in the process of repacking the bundle when *Sardar* spoke again, "Go on, eat well. There are plenty of *paranthas*. Help yourself to some pickle, too.

The bandit with the rifle called out, "There are some onions down there. Take them if you like."

He started eating. The tension in the air seemed to ease somewhat. *Sardar* asked, "Where are you going?"

"I am going to Chindora. From there I'll take a bus," he answered.

"Hmm. You'll reach Chindora by midday." After a while *Sardar* asked again, "Where do you come from? From this village? Jhirka?"

He nodded as he ate on.

The rifleman asked him, "Have you ever heard the name of Daan Singh?"

He choked on his food.

"Daan Singh the dacoit?" He asked.

Sardar offered him a bottle of water and answered, "Not a dacoit, call him Daan Singh the rebel."

"Yes of course — that is what I meant." It was obvious who he was sitting with.

"There is a reward of fifty thousand rupees on his head." *Sardar* was saying, "I am also from the same village as you. My daughter was abducted at the behest of the present Thakur's father."

A long silence followed.

"I broke into his house and cracked open his skull with an axe." *Sardar* spat on one side and continued, "Now his sons are upto the same tricks and we have heard someone called Daani Ram is going to take revenge upon them. He is said to be forming a party." He spat again and carried on,

"The bloke thinks he can destroy him by raising slogans! Bastard! *Saala*, coward! A woman's offspring! He does not have the guts to raise his hand, and thinks he can change the law!"

The train was slowing down. *Sardar* stood up, adjusted the cartridge belt on his waist and addressed the rifleman, "We are approaching the *bada nullah*. Get ready."

Both of them prepared to jump down. Before their exit, *Sardar* said, "Throw away the leftovers after you have eaten. And be warned — do not inform the police!"

Daani Ram stood up for the first time. "Don't worry, *Sardar*. You are from the same village as I. I am from the same stock as you. I am a part of the same *fasal* that has yielded you!"

In a moment the two men jumped off the moving train and into the night. Daani Ram stood and gazed into the darkness for long.

kiski kahani?

It was only after his story was published in the school magazine, that I learnt Annu had an important sounding name — Anil Kumar Chattopadhaya. Class Six.

Annu had always wanted to become a story-writer. He could always spin-out stories. I was convinced that he would become a poet or a writer. Everyone can't be a poet, poetic inspiration is a divine gift. Annu had that rare quality which only a genius has.

Even when we played *gilli-danda*, Annu would sit apart, either lost in thought or busy scribbling in his note-book. I was always curious to know what was going on in his head, how he made his characters come alive, how he wrote about them on the piece of paper before him — how they lived and breathed. Annu sent them wherever he wanted to, made them do whatever he wanted to, and as they moved from place to place, the plot of a story got created — wonderful! Story-writers are marvellous, they can kill whom they want, give life to whom they want. Aren't they like gods?

Annu laughed. We were in college by then, and said, "No, that's not true. My characters are not imaginary, they are not under my control. In fact, I am under their control."

Annu even talked like a writer. I always liked that. I felt very proud when his stories were published in the Sunday editions of *Pratap*, *Milap* and *Jung*.

I showed the newspaper to my mother and said, "See, a story by Annu — Anil Kumar Chattopadhyay. That's his name."

"Really, read it to me."

I read the story to her. It was about a poor cobbler. My mother had tears in her eyes.

"*Arrey*, that is the story of Bhiku, the cobbler in our lane. The same thing happened to his mother."

I didn't know that, but I immediately repeated what Annu had told me, "His stories are not imaginary, Ma. He doesn't create characters, but finds them in real life. To do that one must not only keep one's eyes and ears open, but also keep the windows of one's mind and intellect open."

My mother was very impressed by my speech, which was really Annu's.

There was a very large jamun tree in the lane. Bhiku, the cobbler used to sit under it. He used to repair the shoes of the entire neighbourhood, and it was Annu's favourite haunt. Annu's clothes may have been dirty and unwashed, but his shoes were always well-polished.

Bhiku was teaching his son, Ghasita, how to stitch the toe-strap of a chappal. When I read the story out to Bhiku, his voice choked, and he said, "Son, only people like you can understand our pain. Now if you people don't tell our story, who will?"

My respect for Annu rose further from that day. He was truly a born writer.

After finishing college, I left Delhi and went to Bombay, and got a job there. Annu started helping his elder brother run the *baithak* from where he used to distribute ayurvedic and homeopathic medicines. His elder brother worked in some government office. He used to run the dispensary for two hours every morning and evening. He had recommended Annu for many jobs, but had been unsuccessful in getting him one.

Once, when I went back to Delhi to attend my sister's wedding, I met Annu's elder brother. He was very ill. He said to me, "Why don't you make him see sense? Ask him to do some work. What's the use of writing stories?"

I kept quiet. He coughed and wheezed for a long time. Then he said, "If only that bitch would leave him alone — he would come to his senses."

I asked Annu who the bitch was.

He replied, "Fiction. Bhai Sahib always curses it. He doesn't understand that he treats physical illnesses. I treat social and mental illnesses. I lance the pus-filled boils of society, light the path of people who are lost in darkness. I give them weapons to break the chains of their mental slavery with."

I felt like applauding him. He talked for a long time. He

told me that his first book was ready for publication. Many of his stories had appeared in some of the leading magazines of the country. He often got requests for stories from journals, but he couldn't write for all of them. He had even begun writing a novel but hadn't finished it, because he hadn't found enough time away from the *baithak*. His elder brother who had two children had been ill for some years. Poor souls! He was thinking of writing a story about the children.

During our conversation, he talked about great writers. I had heard of some of them — Saadat Hasan Manto, Ahmad Nadeem Qasmi, Krishan Chander, Rajinder Singh Bedi, but the others he mentioned after that were new to me — Kafka and Sartre. Some of the things he said, about Kafka's symbolism and Sartre's existentialism went above my head. I thought that fiction had been left far behind. But Anil Kumar Chattopadhaya, trying to explain things to me, said, "The importance of a story doesn't merely lie in the development of its plot and the characters involved in it, but in its exploration of the consciousness ... "

I didn't, of course, understand what he said, but I couldn't help being impressed by its profundity.

Anil once came to Bombay to attend a writer's conference. I took out the autographed copies of his four books to show him. I used to feel very proud whenever I showed them to my friends. They were books by an important writer — and now he was staying with me! I asked him if he had finished the story about his elder brother's children.

He gave me the sad news, "Bhai Sahib died. Relatives got together and persuaded me to marry his widow. Now I am the father to his two children!"

Anil stayed with me for a few days, and then left.

I read about him often in the newspapers. Whenever he published a new book, he always sent me a copy.

Years later, I had to go to Delhi again. I took my wife with me. I had promised to introduce her to my friend, the writer.

That evening, Annu was sitting under the jamun tree and getting his shoes polished by Ghasita. That was still his favourite place. We began talking about fiction once again.

"The most important thing about the new kind of story being written is its concern with the changing reality. The real is not only that which can be seen. In fact, reality can't be seen with one's eyes alone. A story isn't merely about logical relationships; it is rather an exploration of the subconscious of the characters."

I listened to him open-mouthed and in silence. Anil Kumar continued to talk.

"During the last fifty years, there have been many changes in Urdu fiction. Our stories have made so much progress that they can be compared with the best in the world ..."

Ghasita said, pushing the polished shoes towards him, "Whose story are you talking about, Bhai Sahib? The people with whom your stories are concerned are still where they were before. I now sit in my father's place, and you run your brother's *baithak*, what story of progress are you talking about?"

Handing over the shoes, Ghasita grew absorbed in stitching the toe-straps of a chappal.

raavì paar

I don't know why Darshan Singh didn't go mad. His father died at home, his mother was lost in the ruins of the Gurudwara, and Shahni had given birth to twins, two sons. He wasn't sure if he should laugh or cry. Fate had made a strange bargain with him — given with one hand and taken away with the other.

They had heard that freedom was coming, but they didn't know when it would reach Layalpur. Both the Hindus and Sikhs had secretly begun to gather in the Gurudwara. Shahni used to groan with labour pains day and night. It was her first confinement.

Darshan Singh used to bring news about the latest riots.

Bhapaji, trying to comfort him, always said, "Nothing will happen, son. Nothing will happen. Has a single house, either of a Hindu or a Sikh, been yet attacked?"

"But, Bhapaji, the Gurudwara has been attacked, hasn't it? It has been set on fire twice."

"And yet all of you want to gather there!"

That always silenced Darshan Singh. People, however, continued to leave their homes and take shelter in the Gurudwara.

"People feel more secure when they are together, Bhapaji. There is no Hindu or Sikh left in our lane. We are all alone here."

Ten or fifteen days earlier, they heard Bhapaji fall in the courtyard one night. They had got up with a start. They could hear slogans being shouted in the direction of the Gurudwara — "*Jo bole so nihal.*" The slogans woke up Bhapaji and he went up to the terrace to investigate. Coming down the steps, he slipped and his head struck against the axe lying in the courtyard.

They somehow managed to complete the last rites for Bhapaji. After that, they stuffed all their valuables in a pillow-case and the three of them sought shelter in the Gurudwara. There were quite a few terror-stricken people there and that is why they felt safe. He was no longer afraid.

Darshan Singh said, "We are no longer alone. And, in any case, *Waheguru* is with us."

A group of young volunteers was busy with work all day long. People had brought with them all the flour, *dal* and *ghee* they had in their homes. The community kitchen was open day and night. But how long could they have lived there? The question troubled everyone. People hoped that the government would send them some help soon.

"Which government?" someone asked. "The British have left."

"Pakistan has been created, but the government of Pakistan is yet to be formed."

"I have heard that the army is out everywhere and is helping migrants to reach the border."

"Migrants? Who are they?"

"Refugees."

"I've never heard those words before."

A group of two or three families couldn't endure the tension any longer.

"We are going to the station. We have heard that the trains are running again. How long can we stay on here anyway?"

"We'll have to be courageous. *Waheguru* can't carry us on his shoulders, can he?"

One of them shouted loudly, "*Nanak naam Jahaz hai, jo chadhe so utare paar.*"

The departure of a few people always left behind a vacuum in the place. It would be filled only when other people arrived and brought news from the outside world.

"There is a huge encampment at the station."

"There are some people who are dying of hunger and others of overeating! Also there is the outbreak of an epidemic."

"Five days ago, a train had passed this way. There was no place on it even for a sesame seed. People were packed tightly on the roofs."

It was Sankranti. Prayers were recited in the Gurudwara from morning till late at night. On that auspicious day, Shahni gave birth to twins. One of them was very weak. There was little hope for his survival, but Shahni struggled to keep him alive.

That night someone announced, "A special train for the refugees has arrived. Let's get out."

A large caravan left the Gurudwara. Darshan Singh joined it. Shahni was very weak, but she agreed to go for the sake of her sons. But Darshan Singh's mother refused.

"I'll come later, my son. I'll come with the next caravan. You take care of your wife and sons."

Darshan Singh argued with her, and the *granthi* tried to reason with her. Then the volunteers consoled him and said, "Leave while you can, Sardarji. One by one, all of us will reach the border. We'll bring Beeji with us."

Darshan Singh left with the others. He placed his children in a wicker-basket and then lifted it onto his head, as if it contained all the wealth of his family.

The train was waiting at the station, but there was no free space in it. People seemed to sprout from the roofs of the compartments like grass.

When people saw the new-born children and their ex-hausted mother, they felt sorry for them and made place for them on the roof.

About ten hours later, the train began to move. The evening sky was red, bloody and hot. Shahni's breasts had been sucked dry. She tried to suckle each child alternately. Wrapped in two dirty bundles, it seemed as though the children had been picked-up from a garbage heap.

The train steamed into the night. After a few hours, Darshan Singh noticed that while one child still moved its hands and legs and occasionally cried, the other was very still.

When he put his hand on the bundle, he realized that the child was cold and had been dead for some time.

Darshan Singh began to weep loudly. People around him realized what had happened. They tried to take the dead child away from Shahni, but she sat like a statue, and clutched the basket to her chest.

"No, he won't drink milk without his brother."

People tried to persuade her, but she refused to let go of the basket.

The train stopped many times, and then started again.

People tried to guess where they were in the darkness.

"We have passed Khairabad."

"I am sure this is Gujranwalla."

"We have another hour to go. Soon after Lahore, we'll reach Hindustan."

Feeling a little more confident, some people even shouted slogans:

"*Har-Har Mahadev!*"

"*Jo bole so nihal!*"

The moment the train reached the bridge, a wave of excitement ran through the crowd.

"We have reached the river Raavi."

"This is the Raavi. We are in Lahore."

In that confusion, someone whispered in Darshan Singh's ear, "Sardarji, throw the dead child into the Raavi. He will be blessed. Why must you carry him to the other side?"

Darshan Singh cautiously pulled the basket away from his wife. And then, he quickly snatched a bundle out of it and, in the name of *Waheguru*, threw it into the Raavi.

In the darkness, he heard the faint cry of a child. Darshan

Singh looked in terror towards his wife. She was clutching the dead child to her chest. Then, a storm of voices arose —
"*Wagah, Wagah.*"
"*Hindustan Zindabad!*"

najoom

Travelling at a speed of one lakh eighty six thousand miles a second and continuing to do so for sixty seconds you will cover crores of miles in a minute.

Light travels at that speed. Travelling at this speed for full three hundred and sixty five days of a year, we'll reach a place from where our earth just cannot be seen.

Continuing the journey and maintaining the same speed for ten thousand light years, we'll arrive at a sun which has been extinguished after burning for crores of years and is about to die out completely except for occasional eruptions out of which flames leap up to a height of twenty to twenty five thousand miles.

Scientific data confirms that the last time this phenomenon occurred its radiance was observed from Earth in 1841 and

1854 respectively.

The shape of that sun is no longer like the round sun we see everyday. It has spread like ink from an overturned inkpot on a *dhurrie*. If you look through a very powerful telescope when the atmosphere is absolutely clear, you could see a spot which looks like the one made by black *jamuns* with which Sikandar often stuffs his shirt pocket on his way back from school.

How far away that sun is! And that sun has a name too. The name is "*Eta Corniae*".

This name was given to the sun by us. Just as the viewers from the world in the outer space must have given a name to our sun.

In the year 1841 in undivided India, the Mughal king, Akbar-e-Sani had just died, four years had passed in a wink and "Zafar" had already ascended the throne.

Poet Ibrahim "Zauq" was the *ustad* to "Zafar" but "Zafar" valued and admired Poet "Ghalib" greatly. And Kalloo, the domestic servant of "Ghalib" used to often tell Munir, "You know, the *Badshah* secretly sends his *ghazals* for corrections and modifications to my master."

"Really?" Munir would respond with wide-eyed wonder,

"I tell you, he does! He may or may not be the *Badshah*, but he too plays upto the famous poets. Big baskets full of mangoes are sent to the house from the royal orchards."

Munir's face would light up like a sparkling cracker. Stars glinting in his eyes, he would tell Kalloo, "Just you wait and see. Mirza Nausha's (Ghalib) star will blaze forth like a torch one day."

Munir was a great admirer of "Ghalib." However, he did

not know him closely. Whenever he saw him he just saluted him by touching his forehead with reverence.

Munir was deeply interested in astronomy. He often asked questions of the people who had knowledge about stars.

"Please tell me something, Hakim Saheb. I have often seen a shooting star but why do the stars move? The pole star remains fixed in the north like God's light to give directions to the moving caravans. But there are those seven stars, the ones recognized as *sapt rishis* by Pandit Shivnath, which are seen above the minaret of the mosque — there," he indicated the direction. "But when I wake up in the middle of the night, I see all seven of them standing guard over my head! I get so nervous. I wonder how and when they come up like that. Wondering what they would be upto next, I fall asleep again. Early in the morning I see them moving towards Jamuna, in the direction of Shahdra."

Hakim Saheb explained with great patience, "Look, Munir *miyan*. The sky you see rises and falls in all its totality. Imagine that you are sitting under a dome and the dome is rotating over your head. All the heavenly bodies, the sun, the moon and the stars are fixed inside the dome. They are the figures which only God can read. He keeps count of them."

"And after Him you can read them, Hakim Saheb," Munir said happily. Hakim Saheb's explanation had pleased him.

Hakim Saheb answered with great humility, "Aztagh-firullah! What am I, *miyan*. I learn only as much as He reveals."

"Remember the night when we saw a falling star blazing through the sky and you had said some great man had departed from the earth? Well, *Badshah* Akbar-e-Sani had breathed his last that day."

"It is like this, Munir *miyan*. When a falling star is seen it is a forewarning of disaster in the direction where it falls. And some famous entity dies in the direction where it has broken from. Now, we did not know that it was the star of *Badshah Salamat* but its blaze indicated that a radiant light had completed its course in the world. As a matter of fact, that star had been glimmering for several days. I had been watching it."

"All these must be the stars of the destiny of God's creatures, then. He must have put numbers on them — some big and some small."

"Yes, of course."

"Do you think I too have a star among them?"

Hakim Saheb paused for a moment and answered reluctantly. "Yes. It must be there." By now he was somewhat bored with Munir's prattle. Resting his head on the bolster, he started fanning himself with a hand fan. Instantly, Munir took it from his hand and started fanning him.

"Well, Hakim Saheb, *Mirza Nausha*'s star must also be present in the sky."

"Hmm." Hakim Saheb had placed his head on the bolster. A post-dinner indolence was already weighing down his eyes.

Munir spoke to him in a conspiratorial tone, "Mirza Nausha is bound to become the *ustad* of the *Badshah* one day. His star would then shine at the place where "Zauq's" is situated at present. The stars must be shifting from place to place according to people's rise in position."

By then Hakim Saheb was fast asleep.

Munir spent part of each night gazing at and trying to

identify the stars.

In the same year, that is 1841, Munir grew restless on spotting a star which was shining brighter than the others. He arrived at Hakim Saheb's house at the crack of dawn and mentioned his discovery to him. Hakim Saheb had not seen it as he had returned from Agra that day and had gone to bed early. Munir had mentioned the star to others, too. Some of them had said they hadn't noticed it but the others said they had.

The same star arose again the next night. It was indeed brighter than the other stars. When it was spotted at the same place on the third night and the others also spoke about it, Hakim Saheb sat up and took note of the event. Munir was highly gratified the day Hakim Saheb acknowledged his greetings and asked him to sit by his side.

"*Arrey*, Munir *miyan*, you have a magnificent vision. I have heard that that star of yours had been talked about in the *Badshah's* court today. The royal astrologer has declared that the ascent of this star over India is an auspicious sign. He has predicted that the fortunes of the Mughal dynasty would take a turn for the better and glory and splendour would be restored to them."

Munir lifted his hands in prayer and said, "*Ameen*," adding, "*Inshallah*, there would be a change for the better in the fortune of our Mirza Ghalib, too. The first anthology of his verse is scheduled for publication next month. All these are signs of happy days to come."

The bright star remained in the sky for a few days and then disappeared. Munir searched hard and waited for its return, hoping to spot it again.

Several years went by. Circumstances in Delhi deteriorated. The British established their supremacy.

Munir got married in 1844. Two or three children were born to him and his wife in as many years. But he did not give up his habit of star gazing at night. It was in 1854 again, that one night he saw a falling star streaking through the sky with a long trail of light following it. In the morning he was on his way to Hakim Saheb's house to inform him of the phenomenon when he learnt that Ustad "Zauq" had passed away. Munir was convinced that what he had seen the previous night was the star of the deceased.

He went and informed Kalloo who ran to tell his master Mirza Ghalib, who was at that moment, busy tending to his half-demented brother.

Another amazing thing happened after a few days. The bright star that he had noticed thirteen years earlier in 1841 had reappeared in the sky exactly at the spot from where Zauq's star had descended from the sky. It shone as radiant as before at the same place for several nights. The same year Mirza Asadullah Khan "Ghalib" became Badshah Bahadur Shah "Zafar's" *ustad* and was honoured with the title of Najmuddaulah Dabir-ul-mulk.

Munir was convinced that he had identified at least one star and he believed that his own star must be situated in the same expanse of the firmament.

mard

She was worried, her pregnancy had begun to show a little. Kappu was about to come home from the hostel. What if he asked her about it? She was scared, even though Kappu was only her son and not her husband, who would ask her for an explanation.

No matter what a woman does, she always has to render an explanation to some man. At times to her father, at other times to her husband or to her son. Baxi had not been required to give an explanation when he had begun to meet Kanta. In fact, if she ever asked him, he would begin to smash the crockery. Sometimes, he would even beat her up. It was during those days, when the tension in the house had increased, that both of them had decided to send Kappu to a boarding school in Nainital, so that he didn't see in the broken crockery, the signs of his home breaking apart. When Baxi met Kanta his attitude towards Rama changed very rapidly. Rama sensed that he would not continue to live with her for long, and that is exactly what happened. The telephone would ring, and then be disconnected at once. Baxi would make a call immediately after that. There would be work at the office during the most awkward hours. She read all the signs — understood them ....

Baxi began to stay away from the house. Official tours were merely excuses. She always knew which hotel he was in, when and where.

Within a year she began to work once again at the bank she had worked for previously. But even then she had to give explanations. To her father and to Baxi. In fact, it was Baxi who had helped her to pacify her father. He knew that it would be difficult for him to run two houses on his salary alone.

Rama's father had taken her aside and asked her, "Is there some problem between the two of you?"

She had firmly told him, "No, Daddy. There are minor problems in any household ... But ever since Kapil has gone to the boarding school, I have begun to feel quite lost."

Her father hadn't questioned her further. He had merely said, "Do send Kapil to meet his *Nana* and *Nani*."

Both of them had replied, "Yes, we shall."

They returned from Kanpur. Both of them had given up asking for and giving explanations. When the matter was out in the open, where was the need for explanations? They decided that they should separate peacefully. Kappu, however, was a problem. How could they tell him, make him understand what had happened between the two of them? After all, he was still a child — just nine years old.

Rama's bank-manager, Raman Kumar, had tried to intervene and persuade them to forget all that had happened. But Rama was aware of the intensity of Baxi's passion. After all, he had once loved her as passionately.

Raman Kumar had even told Rama one day, "I understand why you cry. But I am more surprised when I see tears in Baxi's eyes when I talk to him. He has never uttered a word against you. He even admits his fault. Maybe he is a very emotional man."

She knew that Baxi could sometimes act wrongly, but his tears were not a pretence. He was not a hypocrite.

By the time they filed for a divorce, another year had passed.

In the meanwhile, they went either separately or together to meet Kappu at the hostel. During his vacations they sometimes took him to places outside Delhi, or he stayed with Rama while Baxi went out of Delhi on an official tour.

Kapil, of course, knew that there was something wrong. But he could only bring himself to say, "Papa doesn't love either you or me. as much as he used to."

"Don't be silly! He's much too busy with his office work, that's all." She didn't want to spoil his innocent ways of thinking. "Besides, I have also started working."

After they were divorced, Rama demanded custody of her son. Baxi didn't really oppose her — he gave in. He knew that he wouldn't be able to explain Kanta's presence to his son. It would affect him adversely. Although he continued to go and meet Kappu at the hostel regularly, Rama never told

Kappu about the divorce.

The affair with Kanta too didn't last very long. But after that neither did Rama want Baxi back, nor did Baxi want to return. Their relationship had already broken up. It was no longer possible to repair it. And that year, when Kapil was about to come home during his vacations, Baxi was transferred to Madras a city thousands of miles away from Delhi. Baxi had perhaps forgotten, and Rama found it difficult to carry on with the pretence any longer and she decided to tell Kappu everything. Kappu would be hurt because he was attached to his father. But she would slowly prepare him, talk to him all day about his father and, when she would finally tell him at night, he would weep. She would console him, put him to bed.

"I am with you, son. Your mother ...."

The moment Kappu came home, he asked, "Ma, has Papa left us? Is that true, Ma?"

Rama couldn't control herself. She burst into tears. Kappu came forward and hugged her.

"I am here Ma, I am with you. Your son ...."

She was surprised. How imperceptibly these children grow up, much before one realizes it!

Kappu had returned that day from the hostel after two years. He was now thirteen years old ....

During his vacations the year before he had gone to Darjeeling with the boys and girls from his school. She too had gone out for a few days with Raman. She had taken a holiday after many years. The last time she had gone to meet Kappu during Holi, she had wanted to tell him about Raman. But she had been afraid. She didn't want to create a wrong impression on him — after all he was only a child.

Even that day, she had decided a number of times to tell him. After all, Kappu hasn't yet grown up to be a man. He is still a child. Even if he does notice my swollen belly, he will think that I have put on weight. How would he guess? But this time, I'll actually talk to him about Raman, and if possible, explain to him that we had quietly registered our marriage.

When Kappu came, she hid her pregnancy from him throughout the day, wore loose clothes, didn't let her dupatta slip off her body even once, prepared things for him to eat and drink and decided to begin telling him everything once he was in bed at night.

Suddenly, she heard the sound of a glass breaking in the next room. When she ran in, she saw that Kappu had wounded his hand. A glass flower-vase lay shattered to bits all over.

"Kappu ... ?"

The moment she took a step towards him, he pushed her aside.

"Don't come near me ...."

She stopped. Kappu's voice was choked with tears.

"Are you pregnant?"

Rama's hands and feet turned cold, beads of perspiration appeared on her forehead.

"Whose child is it? Raman Uncle's? A bastard!"

But it wasn't Kappu's voice she heard — it was Baxi's. She felt that it wasn't her son who was speaking, but her husband.

batwara

Sometimes, life runs leaping like a wounded cheetah, and leaves its claw-marks here and there. If you connect these marks, you will see a strange pattern.

In 1984-85, a gentleman from Amritsar wrote a series of letters to me, claiming that I was the brother he had lost during the partition of India. His name was Iqbal Singh and he was a professor at Khalsa College. After receiving a few letters, I wrote to him stating frankly that I was in Delhi with my parents during the partition and that I had lost neither a brother nor a sister. But despite that, Iqbal Singh continued to assert that I was his lost brother. He thought that I had either forgotten the events of my childhood or had never been informed about them. He believed that I was very young when I had been lost while crossing the border in a caravan.

It was possible that the people who had rescued me had never told me the truth, or that I was so grateful to them that I refused to accept the truth. I had even informed him that I wasn't a little boy in 1947. I was around eleven years old. But Iqbal Singh wasn't willing to accept my version under any circumstances. I stopped answering his letters. After some time even his letters stopped arriving.

About a year later, I received a call from Sai Paranjpe, a film-maker in Bombay. She said that one Harbhajan Singh from Delhi wanted to come to Bombay to meet me. She didn't give me a reason, but rather unexpectedly, began to ask me some strange questions about my past.

"Where were you during the partition?"

"In Delhi," I replied. "Why?"

"Just like that."

Sai speaks Urdu fluently and well, but she asked me in English, "And your parents?"

"In Delhi. I was with them. Why?"

She continued to talk to me for some time, but I felt that she was using English to cover-up something because she always talked to me in Urdu, though she called it Hindi. But after a while, she couldn't contain herself, and said, "Look here, Gulzar. It's like this. I am not supposed to tell you, but there is a gentleman in Delhi who claims that you are the son he had lost during the partition."

That was a new story!

Nearly a month later, Amol Palekar, the famous actor in Bombay, called me and said, "Mrs. Dandavate wants to talk to you. She is in Delhi."

"Who is Mrs. Dandavate?" I asked.

"The wife of the ex-Finance Minister in the Janata Government, Madhu Dandavate."

"Why?"

"I don't know. When and where can she call you?"

I had never had any dealings with either Mr. or Mrs. Dandavate. I had never met them. I was surprised. I gave Amol Palekar the telephone numbers of both my office and my home.

The story had begun to take strange turns. I didn't know that it was a part of Sai's story. Amol is a good actor and he played his part well and did not reveal the real reason for his call. I am convinced, however, that he knew the story.

A few days later, Pramilla Dandavate called. She told me that one Sardar Harbhajan Singh wanted to come to Bombay to meet me. He thought that I was the son he had lost during the partition.

It was the month of November. I remember that. I told her that I would be in Delhi from January 10 onwards to attend the International Film Festival and would meet Sardar Harbhajan Singh. She shouldn't send him to Bombay. I then asked her who Sardar Harbhajan Singh was. She told me that during the Janata regime, he had been the Minister for Civil Supplies in Punjab.

I went to Delhi in January. I booked a room in Ashoka Hotel. Someone called from Sardar Harbhajan Singh's place to find out when he could meet me. By then I had figured out that he was a very trustworthy old man. The one who had called was his son.

Courteously, I suggested, "Please, let him not trouble himself. If you can come here tomorrow afternoon, I'll go with you and meet him at his house."

I was surprised to learn that both Sai and Amol Palekar were also in Delhi and that they knew about my appointment for the following day.

The person who came to pick me up the next day was Sardar Harbhajan Singh's eldest son. His name was Iqbal Singh.

Punjabis do not grow old even at an advanced age. When I came face to face with Harbhajan Singh, he got up to receive me with great affection. Like a son, I touched his feet. He introduced me to my 'mother'.

"Son, she is your mother ...."

I touched Ma's feet, too, like a son.

His sons called him Darji. His second son, his daughters-in-law, grandchildren — were all present. His was a big, well-to-do, family. The house was large and spacious. Punjabis not only build big and open houses, they also have large and open hearts.

After we had talked about all sorts of things, some snacks and drinks were served. Then Darji told me when and how they had lost me.

"The riots were terrible. Everything around us was on fire — and rumours added fuel to the flames. But we refused to leave. The *Zamindar* was a Muslim and a friend of my father's. He was also grateful to us for favours in the past. Everyone in the *qasbah* knew that as long as he was around no one could even knock at our door. His son used to study with me in school (I think, he said the boy's name was Ayaz) But whenever caravans of refugees passed through our *qasbah*, we lost heart. We began to tremble with fear. The

Zamindar came every morning and evening. And he never failed to comfort us and instil courage in our hearts. He treated my wife like his own daughter.

"But one day, when a caravan passed through cursing and shouting slogans, we spent the entire night standing on the roof-top to watch it — not only us, but the entire *qasbah*. I don't know why, but we felt as if it was the last caravan. We should leave with it. Nothing would survive after that. We betrayed the trust of our friend, the *Zamindar*, and left.

"He used to tell us, 'Come and live in my *haveli*. Lock up your house for a few days. No one will touch it.'

"But we pretended to be confident and brave. Inwardly, however, we were terrified. To tell you the truth, Sampooran Kaka, our faith had been shattered, our roots had been shaken. All the caravans passed through our place. We had heard that if we entered Jammu via Mianwalli, we would get help from the army to go down the rest of the way.

"We left our house unlocked. The truth is that in our hearts we knew the time to leave our land had arrived. We decided to pick up our things and escape. With two grown-up sons, a daughter (eight or nine years old) and you. You were the youngest. We had to walk for two days to reach Mianwalli. We always found something to eat in the villages we passed through. There were riots everywhere. Gangs of rioters always came from outside. The caravan had grown very large by the time it reached Mianwalli. People came from all directions to join it. Son, the presence of others who had suffered like us, gave us some strength. We reached Mianwalli at night. During our journey, we often lost sight of our children and called out to them in anguished despair. There were others like us, and there was always a lot of crying and screaming.

"That night, I don't know how the rumour spread that the caravan at Mianwalli was going to be attacked. That a large mob of Muslims was on its way — one could sense fear and terror in the silence. All of us left that very night."

Darji fell silent for a while. His eyes were moist. But Ma was looking at me in silence. There was no emotion on her face.

Then Darji said very quietly, "It was during that night that we lost both our youngest children. I don't know how. If we had known ...."

He left the sentence unfinished and fell silent.

I don't clearly remember, but I think his sons and daughters- in-law got up and the others present shifted uncomfortably in their places.

Darji continued his narrative.

"Once we got to Jammu, we waited for a long time. We searched one camp after another and watched every caravan that arrived. There were thousands of people. Some joined caravans going to Punjab, others went down the hills to places where they had relatives. We gave up hope and went to Punjab. We continued to search the camps there. All we could do was to search. The children were lost and we abandoned all hope.

"About twenty or twenty-two years later, a group of pilgrims were scheduled to go to Pakistan from Hindustan. I suddenly felt like making a journey to Gurudwara Panja Sahib. I also wanted to see our old home, but my wife always broke down at the very thought.

"We also couldn't overcome our sense of guilt at the fact that we hadn't trusted our *Zamindar*. Whenever we thought of him, we felt ashamed of ourselves.

"Anyway, we finally decided to go. But before leaving, I wrote a letter to the *Zamindar* and another to his son, Ayaz. I even asked them to forgive us for having deceived them. I told them about the reasons for our *hijrat*, sent them information about my family and also told them about our lost children, Satya and Sampooran. My hope was that even if Ayaz didn't remember us, the *Zamindar*, Afzal, couldn't have forgotten us. I didn't post the letters here, because I thought I would post them once I got across the border. We were planning to be in Pakistan for twenty or twenty-five days, and I was sure that if Chacha Afzal wanted to meet us, he would send a reply. If he invited us, we would go, otherwise — what was the use of digging up old graves? What could be gained by doing that?"

Harbhajan Singhji took a deep breath and continued.

"Those letters remained in my pocket, Punniji — I, somehow, lost heart. But the day I returned via Karachi, I don't know what made me post the letters.

"I waited for a reply, even though I didn't think I would receive one, and after a few months had gone by, I gave up all hope.

"I got a reply after eight years."

"From Afzal *Chacha*?" I asked in surprise. He didn't reply. I asked again, "From Ayaz?"

He nodded and exclaimed sadly, "Yes! In response to my letter. It was from his letter that I learnt that Afzal *Chacha* had passed away a few years after the partition. Ayaz had looked after the land after Afzal *Chacha's* death. Ayaz too died recently. It was when his papers were being examined that my letters were discovered. When one of the persons who had come to stay with the bereaved family read out the letter, someone informed those who were gathered there that the girl mentioned in the letter was present in the house at the moment and had come to offer her condolences from Mianwalli. When she was questioned, she told them that her real name was Satya. She had been separated from her parents during the partition. Now she was called Dilshad."

Ma's eyes were still dry, but Darji's voice was tearful.

"I called upon *Waheguru* and left that very day. I met Dilshad at Afzal *Chacha's* house. And do you know, she remembered everything. But she didn't remember her own house. I asked her how she had got lost? How she had got separated from us? She said, 'I got tired of walking. I was very sleepy. I saw a *tandoor* in a courtyard and went to sleep next to it. When I woke up, I saw that no one was around. I would look for you all day and go back to the *tandoor* to sleep. When the owners of the house came back three days later, they woke me up. Husband and wife. They let me stay there in the hope that someone would come looking for me. But no one came. I stayed there like a servant. They fed me and gave me clothes. They looked after me well — and then after many years, maybe eight or nine years later, the master of the house married me. By the grace of Allah, I have two sons. One is in the Pakistani Air Force and the other has a job in a good firm in Karachi.'

Writers are in the habit of asking a few questions, which are not always necessary.

"Wasn't she surprised to see you? To meet you? Didn't she cry?"

"No. She was surprised, but wasn't too upset," Darji replied. "In fact, whenever I think about her, I see her smiling repeatedly at us, as if I had gone there to tell her a story. She didn't seem to feel that we were her parents."

"And Sampooran? Wasn't he with her?"

"No. She didn't even remember him."

Ma, once again, repeated what she had said a few times earlier during her husband's narrative, "Punni (Sampooran), why don't you believe us? Why do you want to hide from us? You have even changed your name to Gulzar. Just as Satya's name was changed to Dilshad."

After a pause, she continued, "Who gave you the name Gulzar? Your name is Sampooran Singh."

I asked Darji, "Who told you about me? How did it occur to you that I am your son?"

"It's like this, son. When we found our daughter, by the grace of *Waheguru*, after thirty years, we began to hope that He would help us find our son too. Iqbal read an interview of yours in some paper and told us that your real name is Sampooran Singh and that you were born over there, in Pakistan. It was that which persuaded us to look for you. Yes, I forgot to tell you that my son was given the name Iqbal by Afzal *Chacha*."

Ma said, "*Kaka*, you continue to live where you want. It doesn't matter if you have converted to Islam, but please accept the fact that you are my son, Punni."

I repeated, once more, the history of my family and left them feeling hopeless.

The story I have recorded happened about eight years ago. Now it's 1993.

After eight years now, I suddenly received a letter from Iqbal, along with a card for a Bhog ceremony announcing that Sardar Harbhajan Singhji had passed away. Ma, he said, wanted him to inform her youngest son.

I felt as if my own Darji had passed away.

haath peeley kar do

I

Malati was still young in those days — and the bay behind Char Bungalows overflowed with water during high-tide at noon and in the evening. When the bay was filled with water at noon, the van from Super Textiles left bundles of cloth for the washermen at the shore. The washermen, who used to pick them up, would scatter along the shoreline like hens who had suddenly been released from their coops. The driver of the van, Ramnath, would then blow the horn thrice in his own peculiar style — like a signal : "Bee-beep, bee-beep! Bee-beep, bee-beep! Bee-beep, bee-beep!"

It is said that whenever Lord Krishna played his flute, Radha went mad with longing till she found him. In those days, Lord Krishna didn't have a car. Otherwise, he would have saved himself the trouble of playing on his flute.

"Bee-beep, bee-beep! Bee-beep, bee-beep! Bee-beep, bee-beep!"

Malati would turn to her mother and ask, "Ma, can I go to Shiela's place?"

"What's this madness? As soon as it's afternoon, you want to go to Shiela's place!"

"Ma ... I ... I ...."

"Alright, go, don't bother me."

And Radha, lost in the ecstasy of the flute, dancing to its tune, would find Lord Krishna. Ramnath would drive extremely fast and take her to a lonely spot beyond the banks of the Jamuna.

The washermen would look up for a moment, cluck like hens and then scatter once more along the shoreline. One washerman would look at the couple enviously, another would dramatically fall on the sand and sing loudly, "*Peena pilana bhoola gayee ek shahr ki laundiya ....*"

Malati would lie in the car with her head on Ramnath's lap.

"Do you know what Ma said when she heard you blow your horn yesterday?"

"What?"

"She said that it was half past one and when I asked her how she knew, she answered that 'when the washermen gather along the shore everyday in the afternoon and the driver of the van blows his horn like that, the time is one thirty.' "

Ramnath laughed loudly and said, "Tell Ma that instead

of a single horn, I'll arrive one day with an entire band."

Everyday, Ramnath used to drive Malati back to the bay after a few hours. The washermen always looked up, clucked at each other like hens, and went back to work.

Malati went back home. She cleaned the kitchen. When Bapu finished his dinner, she lit his *hookah*. Ma began to massage Bapu's feet. Malati lay down on her bed and began to wait for the high-tide again. During high-tide in the evening, the bay would overflow with water. She could hear the roar of the sea come nearer and feel the waves sweep over her. Her bed seemed to float on the water. She would swim across many seas and reach alien islands. But the moment she opened her eyes, she would find herself back in the same kitchen — the same stove, *hookah*, Bapu and Ma! She would finish her work mechanically and wait for the high-tide.

"Bee-beep, bee-beep! Bee-beep, bee-beep! Bee-beep, bee-beep!"

"Ma, can I go to Shiela's place?"

"What madness is this?"

"Ma ... I ... I ...."

"Alright, go!"

Radha would run until she fell into the arms of Murali Manohar again. One day, just as Malati met Ramnath, she heard a loud scream behind her. It pierced her ear-drums.

"Malati ... !"

Malati swirled around like a whirlpool and freed herself from Ramnath's embrace. Her mother stood before her. She caught Malati by her hair and dragged her back home.

Unable to move, Ramnath continued to sit like a statue.

That night, Malati lay in her bed and wept inconsolably.

Ma, as she massaged Bapu's feet, talked to him for a long time in whispers. Malati only caught one sentence, "Our daughter is no longer a child, find a good home and stain her hands yellow."

All mothers and fathers say the same thing. The same sentence echoes in their ears. Malati lay with her head buried in her pillow and sobbed all night.

That night there was another small tragedy in Char Bungalows. The chowkidar saw a thief trying to scale the back wall of Char Bungalows at night and enter the locality. The people caught him and beat him up mercilessly. When they grew tired of thrashing him, they handed him over to the police. Two days later the man died in police custody. The entire incident was hushed up by the police. A few people who had gone to the police-station to hand over the thief, claimed that he was Ramnath, the driver, who was merely trying to meet Malati.

II

There is a lot of power in flowing water. Rivers can change their course, the sea can carve out a new shoreline, even the bay had receded further from the walls of Char Bungalows. The entire neighbourhood of Char Bungalows has changed. Only Malati continues to live in the same place with her three children — her eldest daughter, Lata, her younger daughter, Leela, and her son, Raju. The hair near her temples has already begun to grey.

The Super Textile Mill shut down years ago. But even

today, when the bay overflows with water at high-tide at noon, a truck from some other textile mill still comes and leaves bundles of cloth for the washermen — but it stands on the beach silently, sadly, as if it too has grown old. The washermen still collect their bundles of cloth and spread them along the shoreline.

Malati's father is no longer alive. Her mother is on her death-bed. Her husband, Bishandas, works at home. He is smoking a *bidi* and embroidering a piece of cloth with gold thread. Whenever he gets tired of working, he fondly calls out to his daughter —

"Lata, *Betay*."

"She is good for nothing. All she does is sleep all day. It seems, she has to plough a field at school everyday." Malati has begun to sound like her mother.

"*Arrey*, why do you get so angry? Children either sleep or cry — and then they suddenly grow up. Lata, *Betay*."

"Coming, Baba."

"*Betay*, please make me a cup of tea."

Lata, still rubbing her eyes, goes to the kitchen and makes him a cup of tea.

Lata is a sensible girl. Bishandas and Malati are very proud of her. It is true, however, that the people of the neighbourhood had once spread the rumour that Lata had started meeting the grocer's son at the corner of the road on her way back from school. But Malati had spoken to them so sternly that they had never again dared to say a word against Lata. Malati was convinced that her daughter would never dare to look at a boy. The question of her meeting a stranger didn't even arise.

"Bee-beep, bee-beep! Bee-beep, bee-beep! Bee-beep, bee-beep!"

Malati, who was in the process of serving food, stopped suddenly. An entire era swept past her eyes in a second. She gasped for breath, and looked around in a daze.

"What's the matter?" Bishandas's voice echoed all around her.

Malati continued to stare outside for sometime. The horn of the van sounded again.

"Bee-beep, bee-beep! Bee-beep, bee-beep! Bee-beep, bee-beep!"

Malati turned around. She ran into the bedroom and saw Lata sleeping peacefully on her bed.

Malati breathed more easily again.

"What's the matter?" Bishandas asked.

"Nothing," she said, as she began to serve him food again. "Nothing. I was just thinking that our daughter is no longer a child. Find her a good home and stain her hands yellow."

michelangelo

Michelangelo had once again been away from Florence for five years. He was beginning to tire of Rome. He couldn't find a face for his painting in Rome. The faces there didn't seem to have any character — they all looked alike. That's what he told Pope Julius II.

"What do you see in my face?" Julius asked.

"A burning candle."

After a moment's pause, Julius smiled. He was used to Michel's caustic comments. "Yes, I understand what you mean. I am like any of those thousands of candles which people light on the altar of the cathedral when they are in trouble."

Michel remained silent.

"I am surprised that in this vast creation of God, where

no face resembles another, you can't find a face for your painting — can't find a model. During the last four months, the face of Judas ..."

Before he could finish his sentence, Michelangelo had walked out of St. Peter's.

Pope Julius was familiar with Angelo's moods. That was Angelo's fifth year in Rome. For five years, he had been painting scenes from the Old and New Testaments on the dome and the walls of the Sistine Chapel. And now that it was nearing completion, Julius didn't want to spoil his relationship with Angelo. Julius remembered that when Michelangelo had carved an image of Jesus in wood for the Church of the Holy Spirit, his model had been a young man who had suddenly died in the monastery. Because of Angelo, they had had to delay lifting his coffin for twelve hours.

Michelangelo wasn't like Bramante who created figures according to rules. That is why the shape and form of Bramante's characters were always the same ... they seemed to belong to the same family. He had dismissed Bramante and once again made peace with Angelo.

Five years ago, when Michelangelo returned to Rome, he used to lie under the dome of St. Peter's for hours and mumble something to himself. Julius began to have doubts about his mental stability. Once, when Julius quietly walked upto him, he heard him repeating verses from the Bible.

"What are you doing?"

"O!" Michelangelo turned to look at the Pope with a start. "I am unveiling the verses from the Bible."

Julius understood him. He was looking for faces in the white-washed brick walls. Jesus's face, Mary's face, Judas's face. The shapes of their bodies were visible, but their faces were hidden in the verses of the Bible.

Michelangelo had drawn many sketches of Gabriel's face on paper. Julius had asked, "How did you draw Gabriel's face? He doesn't belong to this world."

"I heard his voice. In the Old Testament."

"Then you must have also heard the voice of God?" Julius had asked jokingly.

"I have heard His silence."

That had convinced Julius that he had chosen the right artist. "He's an eccentric," he told the Vatican Committee, "but only he can paint the Sistine Chapel."

Michelangelo had chosen his mother as the model for Mary. He had done so on the day he had seen her carry two drums of water hung on a bamboo across her shoulder. Only a woman like her could have carried the weight of the son of God in her womb.

His mother had lit a fire and was heating water for his father's bath. He had closely watched her face glowing in the light of the fire — radiant, warm, brilliant like gold, and made lots of sketches of her face on paper.

That night, as she sat near the stove, he had asked her, "Why didn't you give birth to Jesus?"

"Because I met your father. Look at him lying there inebriated. Go and look after him."

Angelo had immediately made a sketch of his stupefied father on a piece of cardboard and had hung it up next to him, so that his father could see what he looked like when he was drunk. Beneath it he had written, "Father, if you hadn't been like this, Mother could have been Mary."

His mother had liked the sketch very much. She had always kept it with her. "Why don't you carve an image of your father like this. He looks so innocent."

He had always evaded her by saying, "I can't find that piece of marble in which I can see father's face."

That had happened a long time ago. They used to live in Bologna in those days, the pub at the corner of the lane was his favourite haunt. It was also his father's favourite haunt. His father used to drink inside, while he used to take his bottle and sit outside. He used to frequently buy peanuts from a vendor who used to sit across from him. Everytime the vendor weighed peanuts, a few always rolled out of his basket and fell on the ground. Each time a small naked boy standing nearby would pick them up, put one nut in his mouth and the rest back in the basket, and then wait for the next customer. Michelangelo used to buy peanuts just to watch that performance. When he made the statue of the Madonna of Brujis, he used the boy as the model for the naked baby Jesus.

Soon after, the Pope first asked Michelangelo to paint scenes from the Old and New Testaments on the ceiling of the Sistine Chapel. Michelangelo had gone to Rome to meet the Pope because every painter and sculptor in Italy was ready to sacrifice his body and soul to be awarded the commission. It would be enough to win him immortality. But for Michelangelo the mere promise of immortality wasn't enough, he had laid down some conditions for his mortal life here. He need money to buy marble. Pope Julius had promised him some but had later refused to pay him.

"Why do you love stone so much? Why don't you love colours?"

"Colours lose their distinctiveness when used with other colours. They change. Marble doesn't change."

Now he was as tired of colours as he was of Rome.

He only had one panel of the Chapel left to paint — *The Last Supper*, but he drew a blank whenever he tried to imagine one face — the face of Judas the thirteenth disciple of Jesus, who had betrayed his saviour to the Romans for thirty pieces of silver. He had helped to crucify him.

Julius grew more and more impatient.

Michelangelo spent days and days making sketches. He searched through his old drawings and worked on them, but no face satisfied him.

And then suddenly, one day he found Judas in a small, dirty pub in Rome. His eyes had an unnatural glitter, he was restless and he spat again and again. His body had already begun to sag with age. He spoke so fast that words seemed to fall out of his mouth like coins from a torn pocket. He had gone to Michelangelo to beg for a dinar, but had ended up sharing a bottle with him. When Michelangelo came out of the pub, he saw the man ask someone else for two dinars.

Michelangelo made a deal with the man and took him to the Chapel. He told him what he wanted. He wanted him to model for Judas. That would make the man immortal. Michelangelo lifted up the drapes to show him the walls and the ceiling. The man looked at everything with awe. He asked for a large sum of money in exchange for his consent. Angelo agreed to pay him. Then the man asked for an advance which Michelangelo gave. The man came regularly for a few days. Angelo used to call him to the Chapel for sittings. One day, as the man was looking through some old sketches, he asked

Michelangelo about the sketches of the child he had made in Bologna.

"I used to live in Bologna years ago. I used this face to paint Jesus as a child."

"Do you remember his name?"

"Yes ... Marsoleni."

That man smiled. He rolled up his sleeve and showed him a name tatooed on his arm: Marsoleni.

"I am the same Jesus, whom you are now painting as Judas."

bimal da

People call it the day of the holy bath, *Jog Snan ka Din*, which is observed at the confluence of Ganga, Jamuna and Sarswati at Allahabad. It is believed that whosoever takes a dip at the *sangam* that day gets cured of all his illnesses, is absolved of all his sins and lives to be a hundred years of age.

I asked Bimal Da, "Do you believe in all this?"

He answered with a smile, "It is a matter of faith. It is stated in the Shastras."

According to astronomy this day occurs once in twelve years when all nine planets of the solar system come in conjunction in one line and the first rays of the rising sun fall on the *sangam*. That special day is celebrated by holding the Kumbha fair at this spot. Preparations for the fair start months in advance because millions of pilgrims come to it. Big crowds can be seen all the way from Allahabad to Prayag and no accommodation is available in scores of neighbouring villages. The event is recognized as the _poorna kumbha ka mela_. The fair lasts for several days but the last nine days are specially significant out of which the ninth day is the day of the _Jog Snan_.

In 1952 about a hundred thousand people were killed in a stampede at this fair. The real cause behind the accident is still not known. Several inquiry committees have advanced different conclusions. Some people said that the elephants of the _naga sadhus_ had run amok creating panic amongst people. In the melee that followed the temporary wooden bridges constructed by the army and the Home Gaurds collapsed and panic stricken people ran helter skelter and got trampled. Thousands of boats overturned and drowned in the Ganga. It is the worst disaster in the entire history of the Kumbha fair.

Samaresh Basu had written a novel _Amrit Kumbh Ki Khoj_ and Bimal Roy, called Bimal Da by all of us, was making a film based on that novel.

I was an assistant with him at that time. I would also write a song or two for his films but I was the script writer for this film. May be Bimal Da needed a writer who could sit with him at his convenience to discuss and finalize the scenes. Another reason, perhaps, was that I was fluent both in Bengali and Hindi. The original novel was in Bengali but the screenplay was being written in Hindi. Bimal Da was constantly working on that novel during his leisure hours. The margins of the novel were so heavily inscribed with notes and references that his copy seemed to contain another novel between the lines of the original. Notes written on scraps of paper were pinned here and there all over the pages of the book. As it was the size of the novel was immense and all those scraps of paper stuffed into it gave it the appearance of a swollen belly. The novel was pregnant with another novel. It's binding was bursting at the seams. Bimal Da seemed to know each character so closely that "Kumbha" seemed to be an essential part of his being.

"When did you read this novel?" I had asked once.

"In 1955 when it was first published in a serial form. There was this paper, *Anand Bazar*, published from Calcutta. Samaresh used to work with their organization."

"Did you know Samaresh?"

"Hm," Bimal Da answered. He used to speak very slowly and his "hm" was really remarkable. It could convey a thousand meanings. This time I interpreted it as his reluctance to say more on the subject. But he dragged at his cigarette once or twice and continued the conversation.

"Originally Samaresh did not publish the novel under his own name. It appeared under a pseudonym, 'Kaal Kot'."

"Hm," I waited for a while.

He continued, "After about fifteen instalments there was a gap in publication. I felt restless and wrote to *Anand Bazar*. My letter was answered by Samaresh and then I learned... ." He started coughing, rose from his chair and went to the balcony to throw the stub of his cigarette.

The novel did not have a plot but its characters were extremely alive and Bimal Da made me read over and over again parts of the diary of the writer from whose angle the narrative was unfolded. At the beginning of the novel a train, chockful of passengers, leaves Prayag railway station to go to

Allahabad. Only a few minutes' journey remains. People, driven by religious fervour, begin to sing *bhajans*. Passengers sitting on top of the train start thumping the roof shouting slogans. The train glides slowly into the railway station at Allahabad and the crowd of passengers rushes towards the exit as if it is trying to escape from a black hole. Balram, a man suffering from tuberculosis, who was going to be cured of his illness and to obtain a long life at the *Jog Snan*, gets trampled under the feet of the surging crowds and dies.

Bimal Da's objection was, "Samaresh has killed this man too soon!"

I offered my opinion respectfully, "Dada, this lone death gives an indication of the end of the novel and also creates a balance in the narrative."

"Hm ... but it comes too early for a movie. Anyway, we'll see to it later. You carry on, go ahead... ."

It took another three years to go ahead with that script.

The year was 1962. Bimal Da had made two films in the interim, *Bandini* and *Kabuliwala* but work on *Amrit Kumbha* went on. A few small parts were getting shot, especially the ones depicting the fair which could not be recreated artificially. We started shooting them by going to other fairs. Another fair is held at the *sangam* in Allahabad, the annual *Magh Mela*. In the winter of 1962 we started making preparations to film it because two years after that was the next date of the fair of the *poorna Kumbha*.

It was during the preparations for the *Magh Mela* that Bimal Da fell ill. He came to the office with high temperature for a few days as he felt very restless if he stayed away from work.

It was said that he was wedded to films and that he would get the soundest sleep if his pillows were stuffed with the reels of films.

I got worried when he did not come to office for a few days. I went to his house with our senior camera man, Kamal Bose. Bimal Da was sitting in the verandah of his house. A cup of tea and a packet of Chesterfield cigarettes were placed in front of him. He held a lit cigarette in his fingers as usual.

I asked how he was feeling. He replied, "I shall not be able to go to Allahabad. You should all go ahead. Bring back the shots of the fair," and explained the shots to us. He knew almost the entire script of *Kumbha* by heart. He would draw on his cigarette in between explaining the details of the required shots. He coughed and sipped tea as he talked.

Kamal Da remonstrated in Bengali with him and urged him to give up or at least reduce smoking but every time he would just say 'Hm' and resume talking about the script.

Just before leaving for Allahabad we learnt from Ghatak Babu that Bimal Da had cancer.

"Does Bimal Da know it?"

"No."

Ghatak Babu mentioned some tube or pipe in the throat. Kamal Da said, "But cigarette smoking is extremely harmful for that."

"Yes, it is. But Bimal does not listen to me. I wonder how to make him understand. Shall I tell him he has cancer? That he'll die an early death? He gets frightened easily." Sudhesh Ghatak was our manager and he had been a friend of Bimal Da's from his New Theater days.

We took shots of the fair at Allahabad in a half-hearted

manner. We worked efficiently but our hearts were not in it. Our usual enthusiasm was missing. Kamal Da kept very quiet and so did I. There were things we wanted to discuss but we could not bring ourselves to speak about them. The spectre of Bimal Da's cancer was always present at the back of our minds and at a certain mental level we were conscious that shooting was useless and that the film could not be made. But it was extremely difficult for us to accept that Bimal Da would not live for long.

One evening after returning from shooting, Kamal Da asked, "Why is Bimal Da making this film?"

"I had asked him once," I answered.

"So? What did he say?"

I told him about the sitting during which Bimal Da had said, "I have a feeling that I am the writer who had gone in search of *amrit* which makes man live for a hundred years." Surrounded by the cigarette smoke, he had coughed. His face had turned red and after he recovered his breath, he added, "I too have been searching for that *amrit*."

Confused between understanding and not getting his meaning I had asked, "Do you really wish to live for a hundred years?

"Hm."

That day the topic ended at that stage. On another occasion he said, "A hundred years does not literally mean that many years. It means that a man attains immortality through this *amrit*."

"What *amrit* is that?"

Bimal Da had stared far into space for a long time.

Thinking back, now I feel that he knew he had cancer. He

answered at length, "Culture. I want to become a part of the culture of this land so that......" he wanted to say that he should become immortal but he did not say it.

By the time we came back to Bombay, Bimal Da's illness had advanced. However, that untiring film maker had made plans to launch another film whose title, at that time, was proposed to be *Sahara*.

"And what about *Amrit Kumbha*?" I had asked.

"That will be made as planned. In 1964, the twelve year cycle will be complete and the *poorna Kumbha* fair would take place again. We'll complete the film after that.

1964 was still far and it was obvious that Bimal Da did not have much time. *Sahara* was launched. Shooting was done for three or four days. One day he left the set to go home and never returned. The cancer started galloping suddenly and he had to give up his cigarettes. He had realized what his disease was. Tests were conducted in some hospitals after which he was taken to London for treatment. Soon he came back disappointed.

"I want to die at home." He had told someone. A little over a year passed by between his endurance and struggle. The office remained closed often. The unit tried to start a film with the title *Do Dooni Char* but the effort was half-hearted and the work sporadic. Working in a strangely ominous atmosphere everyone knew that the news of Bimal Da's death could come anyday. Experiencing a kind of fear and foreboding, we were gripped by a peculiar helplessness.

Bimal Da sent for me one day. He asked, "Are you working on the script of *Amrit Kumbha* or not?"

I got confused and disoriented. Looking at him, I wanted

to cry. Physically he was reduced to a very small size and he looked like a cushion placed in a corner of the sofa. You could lift him with one hand.

He was annoyed, "I had told you that Balram's death is much too early. Lift that scene from the original place and take it to the fair. He dies on the first day of the nine day *puja*."

I kept quiet. He continued, "From tomorrow, we'll discuss the script every evening. The *poorna Kumbha* fair is scheduled for this year. It is going to start in December."

I said, "Yes it is. The nine day *puja* will commence on 31st December. The day of the *Jog Snan* will fall in 1965."

After his usual "Hm" he remained silent.

After making necessary changes in the script I went to him the next day. By now he knew the script by heart. He sent for his copy of the novel. The binding of the book had gone and the pages were coming loose. He discussed a few scenes and reverted to Balram.

"Move Balram's death further down the script. This is still too early."

I indulged in a little argument out of consideration for his feelings. He told me firmly, "As a matter of fact, you should bring in the death after the writer and Shyama are parted from each other on the fifth day of the *puja*. And when we are shooting at the fair, remember.... ."

Bimal Da would plan the shooting schedule while we finalised the script. Ghatak Babu was given a lot of instructions and he jotted them down with obedient attention.

After two or three days the timing of Balram's death was changed again. It had now been moved from the first part of the script to the last sequence, but Bimal Da was still not satisfied. During a debate lasting two or three months Balram would die two days before or he would get a respite for another four or five days. At any rate, his death was being pushed forward by slow degrees. When I visited him unexpectedly one day he said happily, "I have finally discovered the right place for that scene. On the day of the *Jog Snan*, at the crack of dawn as the first ray of the sun falls on water......then...." he coughed excitedly. His whole body racking by the cough, he continued, "That is when this death occurs. This first death would balance the stampede in the climax. Balram would die on the day of the *Jog Snan*."

I agreed with him and so did Ghatak Babu. Bimal Da looked very enthusiastic. He said, "Give me a cigarette, Sudhesh."

"Why, what has happened suddenly?"

They were talking in Bengali. Bimal Da said, "*Arrey* give it to me, do!"

"No, no. You won't get a cigarette."

"Why? What can it do?"

"I am telling you, it is forbidden. Doctor's orders," Ghatak Baba said firmly.

I could see tears of helplessness poised in Bimal Da's sunken eyes. The tears that could neither spill out nor go back shimmered in his eyes. I couldn't bear it anymore. I excused myself and left and did not go back again. I just could not bear to see him in that state anymore. I had also become like others. There was a fear. A foreboding.

1964 was fast drawing to a close and so was Bimal Da's life. He had stopped getting out of bed. Ghatak Babu stayed with him till the very end. He slept in an extended arm chair in Bimal Da's room.

Ghatak Babu told us about the night Bimal Da passed away. "Woken up by the sound of coughing, I noticed that Bimal Da was sitting up on his bed and smoking a cigarette.

'What are you doing?' I asked.

'I am smoking a cigarette,' he answered coolly.

"I did not try to rise from my chair but motioned him to stop. He said, 'What will happen? Giving up smoking has not helped me so resuming it won't harm me.'

"He coughed again and went out of breath. When he recovered his breath I said again, 'That is enough, Bimal. Fling off that cigarette. Please don't smoke.'

'Why, it is not the first day,' he countered. 'I have been smoking for ten days. You are trying to intimidate me just because you woke up today!'

"Bimal enjoyed his cigarette at leisure and fell asleep. He fell asleep forever. He never got up again."

I got the news in the morning and it was like having the sword of Damocles hanging over my head removed. The moment it went and I recovered my breath, tears poured out of my eyes. It was 8th January 1965, the day of the *Jog Snan*."

zindagi

"Why should anybody cry for me? My troubles are my own. I am free to laugh or cry over them as I please." His silence was the essence of Samir's self. When at age eleven his right arm was amputated the ones to scream were his parents. He had quietly gazed at the faces of those who had come to inquire after the heath of the only child of Raja Saheb.

"No one cried for me," he wrote with his left hand in his diary at age twenty-two. "People cried for the sake of my mother. They cried over my father's misfortune because his only child's arm had been amputated. God had given him only one son who too had lost an arm ..."

However, Samir carried on all his work as usual. The day the bandages were taken off his right arm, he started using his left as if the other one had never even existed. People were amazed at the morale of the boy. They wondered how he endured everything as if nothing had happened.

"My limbs exist because I do. I do not exist by them. I am here. I am alive! So what if my legs are growing weak. I can still crawl on my chest."

Another accident had happened after a few years following the surgery over his arm. He was twenty at that time. He used to go riding with his father every day. But one day, in spite of his father's best efforts to steady him, he fell off the horse and broke his spine. Another operation was performed on him. God knows what kind of metal plates were used by the surgeons to set the bone but as a consequence Samir lost the use of his legs.

People crowded around him once again. Everybody showed their concern. Once again Samir Singh watched their faces in silence.

"Why do they cry? I am not exactly dead. Is it necessary that you walk on your feet? A man can move around even if he does not have legs."

Samir managed to move around, though not on his feet. He kept himself occupied. Tutors came to the house to teach him but when he got fed up of studying, he stopped them from coming. The house had a library. He had it opened. He devoured all the books in a few months time. More books were added to the library. He started writing a diary and he said nothing to the others. He talked only to himself and stayed alive with all his hurts in silence.

After about a year and a half, a new disease developed in his legs. The visits of the doctors were resumed. Some expressed the opinion that the surgery on his spine was not performed properly. The others said it was a new condition in which blood supply to the legs was being obstructed. During those days Samir had made the following entry in his diary.

"So what? I can still crawl on my chest. I can live on my voice. I can go on for long years in my silence."

However, it was Raja Saheb whose condition took a turn for the worse after that incident. He was demented with worry and concern about his son. There was no doctor, *vaid*, *pir*, or *faqir* that he did not consult about Samir. Samir's mother gave up trying to take care of both of them. Shortly after, extreme grief became the reason for her death. Raja Saheb started hovering around Samir like one possessed. He tried to find friends for him but Samir lived within himself. He existed in his own silence, in his own entity.

"My limbs exist because I do. I do not exist by them. I am still alive."

One fine day Raja Saheb suddenly announced that he wanted to arrange a marriage for Samir. He was not worried about the caste or social position of the future bride. All he wanted was someone who would have sympathy for Samir — someone who would be a companion for him for life.

Samir argued with his father and tried hard to resist this preposterous proposition but ultimately he fell silent on seeing his father's mental state. He did realize that his father's grief was greater than his own hurts.

A number of young girls were identified but proposals came from none. Samir wrote in his diary, "People come here for the sake of Raja Saheb, for the sake of his *haveli*, his wealth. As for me, I am just an excuse for them to shed a few tears."

As he was about to give up the quest, Raja Saheb received a proposal. The young woman was from a good caste and she had the right attitude. One glance at her, and Raja Saheb was convinced that she had agreed to marry Samir because she understood his pain and not because she was enamoured by his wealth.

Preparations for the wedding started. Raja Saheb left no stone unturned to make it a grand success. People were awe-inspired at his extravagance. Whispers went round, "He is not a father — he is as generous as a mother!" Raja Saheb fulfilled all the aspirations and desires of his late wife with regard to their only son's wedding. He did as much for the daughter-in-law as for the son. An elaborate *mandap* was set up and bands played lovely music. Fireworks lit up the sky robbing the moon of its lustre.

But by next morning, the parting in the hair of the bride was stained with ashes instead of glowing with vermillion.

Samir had committed suicide.

He had made an entry in his diary. "It would have been better if people cried over me. My ego came to the fore when they pitied me. But what should I do now? People have started laughing at me!"

lɛkɪn?

Devraj suddenly pulled me by the arm and said, "What are you doing? Can't you see the train coming? Didn't you notice the signal?"

I realized then that the situation had got out of hand ...

There was no railway station at Udan. There used to be one. Now, there were only the skeletal remains of the building. But I had seen it full of hustle and bustle once. In those days a chemical plant was being constructed nearby — the railway tracks had been laid for it and goods used to come by train. People, too. Although the plant had been shut down later, the small settlement near the station had remained.

Now the last station on the line was not Udan, but Panvel. About five miles away. The settlement, however, had continued to grow slowly.

I used to go for a walk towards the ruins of the Udan railway station. Wild plants and grass grew on both sides of the railway tracks. The building of the station was utterly desolate — the remnants of the station-master's room, the godown, the small awning, a few cement benches ... somehow, a window had survived. It was obvious from its condition that commuters had once bought tickets there — and there had been a ticket-collector around too. The gate, too, was still intact and its grill-frame was firmly embedded in a cement wall.

I met Devraj there once ... sitting on the cement bench next to the gate. He turned around to look at me when I lit a cigarette. His face was very calm. I thought that he didn't approve of my smoking.

Afterwards, I saw him quite often. Once or twice, he got up and left before my arrival. More often, he waited until I left.

Then, one day, I didn't go there. I had to go to Bombay in connection with my pension. I got back late.

When I went there the next day, Devraj got up from his bench, walked along the rusty tracks covered with grass, and came up to me.

"You didn't come here last evening?"

"No, I returned late from Bombay."

"I see." He smiled and walked out of the station. He paused for a moment near the gate and then disappeared.

A few days later, I couldn't go for my evening walk towards the station as it was raining.

The next evening, Devraj asked me, "Why didn't you come last evening?"

"It was raining."

"I see ... Did you know that the train came last evening?"

"What?" I looked at him in bewilderment.

"Yes ... When I learnt that the train had arrived, I knew that he would come too."

"Who?" I asked.

"My son, Shyam. He came by the 7:50 train. I recognized him as he was showing his ticket to the collector."

That evening, Devraj went away with a smile on his face. He left me puzzled — if the 7:50 train had reached Panvel, then ... But what did he mean when he said that he had recognized his son while he was showing his ticket to the collector? I thought that the old man had lost his mind, that there was something wrong with his head.

The next day, I was walking between the railway tracks, when Devraj came up from behind and began to walk beside me.

"I am a bit late today ..." he said.

"Yes ..." I replied and then kept quiet. But I couldn't restrain myself and finally asked him, "Did you meet Shyam last evening?"

"Yes ... over there," he pointed towards the gate and smiled, "when he was showing his ticket to the collector. I recognized him. I knew he would come one day."

When he saw the look of surprise on my face, he added, "Perhaps, you think that this old man is mad — isn't that so?"

I nodded in reply.

"Of course, I know that no train comes here anymore. But it did once upon a time. At 7:50 sharp. I used to come here to receive him everyday. Then, there was an accident one day.

You may have read about it in the newspapers. A man, who was crossing the tracks, fell under the wheels of the train. His body was picked up in three parts. That man was my son, Shyam."

I was stunned. We continued to walk in silence for a while. Then I asked, "Are you sure that he fell under the wheels of the train ... and was killed?"

"Yes ..."

"And yet, you wait for him? You even think that you have met him?"

"Yes. Everything is an illusion. Life and death. Both are illusions. We emerge out of one deception and fall into another deception. And we call that which is real, an illusion — *maya*."

"What is reality?"

"Search ... hope ... wait."

"Search? For what?"

"For time! Which is eternal."

"Time? But time always passes ..."

"That which passes, isn't time. You and I are transitory, time is eternal. Or rather, it passes and is yet eternal."

"But when life comes to an end ..."

"Time never comes to an end," he said, interrupting me. "Life comes to an end ... Time passes, it always passes ... but it never comes to an end."

After a brief silence, I asked, "Have you read Krishnamurti?"

"Yes," he replied. "U.G."

I realized then that he had been influenced by U.G's philosophy.

Then, he asked me in turn, "Have you read U.G.?"

"No. I asked you about J. Krishnamurti."

"You should also read U.G."

"Do you have any of his books?"

This time, he was silent for a while. Then he rummaged through his pocket and pulled out an old visiting card.

"Come over to my place sometime and borrow it."

His name was printed on the card:

Devraj
6/9, B.P. Colony
Udan, Bombay.

Suddenly, he pulled me by the arm and said, "What are you doing? Can't you see the train coming? Didn't you notice the signal?"

We continued to walk up to the old signal. I realized then that the situation had got out of hand ...

After that, I didn't go in that direction for two days. I actually waited for him there on the third day, but he didn't turn up. Nor did he come on the fourth and the fifth days ...

I had to go to Delhi on some work. I just couldn't stop myself I had misplaced his card. But I knew his address by heart: 6/9, B.P. Colony.

A young man opened the door. I don't know if my face revealed anything. But he welcomed me in without questioning me. He said, "Please, come in."

Devraj's photograph was hanging inside. There was a garland around it. My heart missed a beat. Had he passed away?

I asked, "Whose photograph is that?"

"My father's."

"What is your name?"

"Shyam Chander Devraj."

"Oh — !"

"Whom do you want to meet? I thought you were Shobha's tutor."

"No ... I don't know how to tell you, but ... I had come to pick up a book by U.G. Krishnamurti. Your father had once asked me to and ..."

"Oh, I see. His books are locked up in a trunk. If you can come back another day, we'll pull it out for you. Was it yours?"

"No. Let it be ..." I stood up. "The book was merely an excuse. Actually, I wanted to meet Devrajji. But I didn't know that he had ..."

"Yes ... yes ..." Shyam's face was a little pale.

I picked-up courage and asked, "When did he die?"

"Three years ago. He fell under the wheels of a train at Udan station ..."

My head spun.

In order to take hold of myself, I left at once. My legs shook uncontrollably ... The steps going down seemed to be endless.

hisab kitab

Babu Dina Nath arranged the marriage of his son, Sarvan Kumar, to Usha, Master Ram Kumar's daughter.

Master Ram Kumar was very happy. He had educated his daughter and had encouraged her to get a B.A. degree. He had also filled her with high ideals. And the best part of it was that when Usha had asked for permission to work, he had not raised the slightest objection. If he was anxious, it was only about one thing — that she would find a husband of her own choice. She was, after all, still very young. Children don't become sensible merely by growing up physically. Usha, however, never gave him any cause for complaint. In fact, whenever the question of her marriage came up, she always bowed her head and said respectfully, "I shall accept your decision."

Usha had been working for three or four years and had taken over the financial burden of the family. But the thought that she was still unmarried had slowly begun to weigh heavily on Master Ram Kumar. She had received many marriage proposals, but the negotiations had always broken down. Everyone demanded money. If someone wanted twenty-five thousand rupees in dowry, another demanded a lakh. Those who didn't need cash, asked for a scooter or a car for their sons.

"Gold and diamonds are, after all blessings ... Besides, it's your daughter who will wear them ... Ultimately, she will use them ... To tell you the truth, Masterji, who doesn't go through good and bad times ... When the times are bad, it's the blessings of one's father and mother that help one ..."

Master Ram Kumar felt that termites had eaten through his brain. He couldn't figure out what to do. Had it been a matter of five or ten thousand rupees, he could have borrowed the amount from someone and averted disaster, but the dowry asked for was beyond his means. He had spent the money he had earned on Usha's education. All he now possessed was the small house in which they lived. If he moved out of it, he could raise the money, but then he wouldn't have a roof over his head.

It was by chance that he met Dina Nath. He had a small shop for painting sign-boards. His business was good. The names of roads were changed every other day. He had useful contacts in the municipality. He greased a few palms and got the orders. When streets get new names, how long does it really take to forget the old ones? There was also no dearth of names and numbers of houses and shops to paint. Four or five people worked for him, and his only son looked after the business well. Never was an English alphabet painted incorrectly. And now, he even had an English-Hindi dictionary at the shop.

Master Ram Kumar came to the shop to get a sign-board painted for his school. There he met Dina Nath. He had got the words for the sign written in chalk in a beautiful hand. Dina Nath wanted to know who had written them.

"My daughter. She used to draw at school."

"Really, what does she do now? Study?"

"She's a graduate. She has a job."

"Good, very good."

When Master Ram Kumar went back to pick-up the board, he had a long talk with Dina Nath.

He was delighted with Dina Nath's way of thinking.

"I am completely in favour of allowing girls to work. They should get out of the kitchen and see the outside world — in fact, I think, they should not only stand on their own feet, they should also walk and run. Now take our house. If Sarvan's mother wants to come to the shop from her house, one of us has to go and fetch her. We spend twice the amount on the fare. Isn't that old-fashioned, Master ... Master Ram Kumarji?"

Both of them got along well.

One day Dina Nath went to have tea at Master Ram Kumar's house. He also met Usha.

Another day Master Ram Kumar was invited to dinner at Dina Nath's place. Usha went with him. The two families were happy to meet each other.

And then, one day ...

Babu Dina Nath arranged his son, Sarvan Kumar's marriage, to Usha, Master Ram Kumar's daughter.

Both of them were very happy.

Master Ram Kumar said to his daughter, "Babu Dina Nath is a man of high ideals. In this day and age one can always find a husband, but can one get a father-in-law like him? He told me — 'I don't want a single paisa in dowry. Send the girl in the clothes she's wearing. Your daughter will have complete freedom to continue with her job.' I was very surprised. He added, 'In fact, my one condition is that Usha should continue with her job when she comes to this house. I don't want a slave in the kitchen ...' "

And, Dina Nath, trying to console his wife, said, "Don't be angry, *Bhagyawan!* Do we still have any of the gold you brought? Some of it was used to build the shop and the rest to pay the taxes. I have brought gold which lives and breathes — pension and dowry rolled into one. She earns fourteen hundred rupees a month and she also draws well. We can save twelve hundred rupees by firing a worker. Isn't that so?"

guddo

At times she had herself felt that she was older than her age. When she was in standard eight she talked like girls who were in the tenth. When promoted to standard nine she began to feel as old as a college student, like Badi Didi. She had started writing a diary and had also grown moody like her. She spent hours preening herself like Badi Didi in front of the mirror. She would feel hurt when Ma objected to that.

"She says nothings to Didi but I get shouted at for everything," she would grumble to herself and fall silent.

However, she exploded the day Didi stitched a new frock for her.

"I am not going to wear a frock. How come you buy such beautiful sarees for yourself, but for me you have made this lousy frock!"

"When you grow up, Guddo, ..."

"Don't call me Guddo. That is not my name."

"Alright Kusumji, we'll get you sarees when you grow up."

"Am I a small child now? l study in standard nine!"

Didi burst out laughing and Guddo stormed out of the room.

She wondered on what counts Didi considered herself a grown up. She wrote a better diary than Didi. She could utter more effective sweet nothings. Devraj isn't such a good looker either. His nose is too prominent and his hands collide awkwardly when he wipes perspiration from his brow! And what about the one she herself loved? He was the beloved of millions. A real filmstar. Devraj only copied her heart throb. He copied his hairstyle. For a moment she felt that even Didi was nothing, and Didi and Devraj were not a patch on herself and Dilip Kumar. This thought brought her great comfort. Lost in a reverie she melted into Dilip Kumar's arms and started sewing together the floating clouds scattered on the sky.

She had played truant from school on so many occasions to meet her beloved. She had seen *Madhumati* when she was in standard seven or eight.

"*Hai*, how handsome he looked in a full-sleeved sweater in that movie!" she sighed. She would have run to the screen and held his hand if she could! She decided to knit and present a full-sleeved sweater to Dilip when she met him. And on seeing him dressed in a *dhoti-kurta* outfit in *Naya Daur* she was further divested of her senses! She was completely besotted that day. The sight of Dilip perched on the shaft of a tonga and waving his whip in the air was enough to turn her knees to jelly, so much so that she was afraid she would fall in a swoon any moment. At times she found herself rocking along with the movement of the speeding tonga. Not only that but she also supported the broken bridge from below with all her might when Dilip rode thundering across it. She had realized what she was doing only when her friend sitting on the next seat cried out "Ouch!" and pulled her hand out from her grip .... But why has this fat Vyjanthimala got after him? Suddenly she was overcome with feelings of hatred and anger towards Vyjanthimala.

"Dhanno indeed!" she jeered silently. However, what brought her consolation was that Vyjanthimala dies at the end in *Gunga-Jamuna*.

Rising from her reverie, she left the bed and took out a diary from the drawer of her table. A small booklet about *Gunga-Jamuna* was lying between the pages of the diary. The cover of the booklet depicted a photograph of Dilip Kumar and Vyjanthimala. Taking out a pair of scissors from Didi's cupboard, she snipped away Vyjanthi's picture, crumpled it and flung it out of the window. Then she kissed Dilip's picture and touched his hair softly. Keeping the remaining picture tenderly between the pages of her diary she closed it and kept it on the bed. Placing her head on it she again went into her dream world, where only she and Dilip existed. She started weaving together the scattered clouds floating on the sky.

She had been trying to join them together for so long but the clouds kept coming apart. They would neither send rain nor come together in one big whole. How long could she go on doing that? She wished it would rain hard just once so that her passion could cool down.

"How I wish Dilip would write a letter to me," she thought, "just as Devraj writes to Didi."

"But what is Devraj? He is nothing. No one can even attempt what Dilip would write." Hasn't she heard all those letters written by him in the movies?

She opened her diary and started writing another letter to Dilip.

Immediately after her annual exams were over dawned the day she hadn't even imagined in her wildest dreams. On getting up in the morning she discovered that her uncle had come visiting and he was taking everybody to watch Dilip Kumar shooting for a film. It being a school holiday, there was no hurdle in the way. She told *Mamaji* she too was coming.

"Yes, of course," said her uncle, "you are coming with us."

"But what would she do at the shooting?" Didi asked.

"Guddo? She'll take autographs," *Mamaji* had answered.

"Don't call her Guddo, *Mamaji*, she'll get angry. Don't you know that she has grown up now?" Didi was laughing. Guddo was annoyed with her. She thought to herself, 'Let them see how grown up I am when Dilip looks at me with eyes full of love!' She went in and sat at the dressing table and stared at her image.

Dilip and Vyjanthi were rehearsing a scene when they arrived at the shooting. Guddo stood timidly on one side. Holding Vyjanthi's hand, Dilip was saying, "No power on earth can snatch you away from me, Lata. You are mine for ever and ever. Tell me, will you come with me, Lata?" In response Lata placed her head lovingly on Dilip's chest.

"Shameless woman!" Kusum muttered under her breath.

After the shot was over, *Mamaji* said, "Come Guddo. Come, take the autographs."

"No. I don't want the autographs," she said tearfully.

"*Arrey*, what is the matter? What happened?"

"Nothing," she answered and walked out.

Back home, she went straight to her room. She took out her diary from the drawer, pulled out all the pictures of Dilip Kumar from it, crumpled them up and tossed them out of the window.

"Go, go to your Dhanno. Go away, you too."

And collapsing on her bed, she burst into uncontrollable tears!

addha

Everyone called him 'Addha' which literally means one half of something. Neither *poora* (full) nor *pauna* (three quarters), he was just Addha and the name referred to his height. He was very short. No one knows who gave him that name. Had his parents been living, he would have asked them for an explanation.

From the time he could remember he had been called by this name. It is not that it had ever hurt him. He did not mind it at all. He was a happy go lucky chap. When the melon-seller said, "Keep an eye on my shop, Addhey. I'll be right back after eating my lunch," he would cheerfully take his place and waving a wand in his hand, call out, "Come, buy these melons. They are as sweet as lumps of sugar."

He took turns selling melons and dates. He cheerfully ran

errands for various people. He would fetch medicines from Vaidji for Nani, drop Keshwani's little daughter who lived on the third floor to school, and whenever Madho *mistri* was short of labour he would carry bricks for him. But what he loved most was to dance at the head of a *baraat*. It did not matter whose *baraat* it was. Every wedding procession passing within a mile of the area where he lived would have him swinging his arms and shaking his tiny legs and dancing away to glory right in the front. As was his wont, he stepped forward dancing to join the *baraat* of Ilyas, the silverleaf maker. Pandit tried to stop him, "*Abe* Addhey, how come you are dancing in the *baraat* of a Muslim?"

Slicing the air with both his hands, he replied, "Drums are beaten in the *baraats* of both Hindus and Muslims. And they are beaten in exactly the same manner!"

Playing with twelve-year-old children, Addha looked their age. During the children's school hours he assisted the gardener of the society in sweeping and collecting dry 'neem' leaves and at night he set them afire with matches borrowed from the house of Professor saheb.

On one occasion the Professor gave him an old coat. Coming out, Addha examined it and handed it over to Mali *chacha* saying, "He has given me a great big sack. Three of my size can easily fit into it !"

The eighty families residing in the five buildings of Chhatrapur society had about three and half hundred members collectively. Addha spun like a top amongst them. Nothing came to a standstill without him but the fact was that he was indispensible in many ways. They were kind of incomplete without him. Addha seemed to have added to the

Chhatrapur society like a pet cat whose presence enhances a family consisting of several members.

But yesterday he had gone leaving all of them feeling poor and shallow. The Professor had shouted at the crowd assembled in the compound of the society, "You are incomplete — you are half men, and look, how complete, how integrated is the person you call Addha!"

It happened yesterday but the thing had started two years ago. Actually something had occurred even before the real thing and that was not any less important. But very few people knew about it.

That day Radha Kamalani, the prettiest girl in Chhatrapur society happened to be walking through the Heerganj area when she was surrounded by three goondas. The first of them winked at her, the second blew a wolfwhistle and the third scraped her shoulder as he overtook her. She was petrified but noticing a shadow at the far end of the street she screamed, "*Addhey* !"

He came running in response to her scream. Radha held his hand and said, "Please take me home, *Addhey.*"

He grasped the situation in no time and reacted with the courage of a lion. Holding Radha's arm he said, "Let us go. I am here to help you."

He rescued Radha from those three goondas with effortless ease.

However, he could not sleep that night. For the first time it occurred to him that he was twenty-eight years of age. He stopped playing with the children from the next day and started wearing properly ironed clothes. Others noticed the transformation and so did Radha. She just laughed saying

"How cute!"

Addha seemed to have found the new vocation of his life. That of the protector, the bodyguard. Radha liked it. He walked with her to college in the mornings. Sometime he also carried her books. Occasionally he would go to her college in the evening so that she could return with him. But one day Radha broke his heart. She used to go to meet Jagdish and Addha would leave her there. However, Jagdish did not like that. When he objected, Radha reproached him, "*Chhi*! Are you suspicious of him? Of this half of a man?"

Addha could not bear to listen to anything more and left. The moment he came back he started beating a dog lying in the street really hard. Afterwards, he went and lay down in his *kholi* as if he was himself badly injured.

The next day his attitude was changed. People who wanted him to run errands for them were astonished to hear him say, "Will you pay me?"

"Pay you? What will you do with the money?"

"I'll do whatever I like."

Over a time his trunk started showing a collection of coins and currency notes of various denominations.

That was before the real thing. The real thing is that Radha got married after six months. Loud music was playing at her house and you could also hear the band approaching from the corner of the street. Addha could not bear it. His hands and feet which loved to dance started trembling. He got up quickly. Opening his trunk, he took out all the money, went to the flat #13 of Chhatrapur society and knocked at the door.

The occupant of flat #13 was Satya. She lived alone and

had a dubious reputation. Most of the residents of the society wanted her to leave because a large number of men from among them had been seen entering and leaving her flat at odd hours of the night. Addha was aware of that. He did understand everything but had remained quiet, and today...!

We don't know what transpired inside the flat but Addha emerged after full seven hours from Satya's house. By that time the wedding was over and Radha had already left for her married home.

Subsequently, Addha started visiting Satya frequently.

People were very upset that Satya did not refrain from having relations with Addha. What they found most intolerable was that the woman with whom they had relations should also be entertaining the dwarf. So what if she was a hooker!

The whole society grew hostile to Satya. A couple of young men went to the extent of bashing up Addha. He was enraged. Even after the beating he did not refrain from going to Satya's house. She was lying on her bed. May be she was unwell, he thought. Addha stated in a direct, straightforward manner, "Satya, I want to marry you."

Satya caste a glance at him, uttered a faint 'hmm' and turned over to the other side.

Addha held her by the arm and forced her to face him. He said, "Why can't you marry me? Am I not a man? Do you too think that I am only one half of a man?"

Satya looked long at him and said, "Please let me sleep. I am not feeling well."

Satya's arm fell out of Addha's grip. "All right," he said. "Damn you! Go to hell." He turned round, slammed the door and climbed down the stairs.

Actually even this is not the real story because Addha stayed for a year in the Chhatrapur society after this incident. Rumours floating about Satya continued to reach his ears. He had started avoiding walking by 'C' building. Somebody told him that Satya had given birth to a child. The residents of the society could not tolerate that and they had got after Satya's life. "Throw her out, have the flat vacated" was the general outcry.

In spite of such resistance Satya had stayed put for six months.

It so happened only the day before that Addha entered the compound carrying a bag of groceries on his back. He noticed a large crowd near the "C" building. He didn't ask anyone but was told Satya had consumed poison.

On hearing the news he shot upstairs quite forgetting that he was carrying a bag of groceries which he could have taken off his back. Somehow, people gave way to him till he reached flat #13. He saw Satya lying dead on her bed. A six-month old baby was playing with the corpse.

The Professor's voice was echoing all through the compound, "One of you is the father of this child. You have all been visiting her. I know you have enough decency to contribute money towards her cremation ... but this child.... I ask you, who is going to accept him?"

All stood petrified.

Suddenly the bag of groceries slipped off Addha's hand. People watched him intently as he stepped slowly towards the bed, picked up the child and held him to his shoulder without looking at anyone. Turning around, he walked through the crowd and went out of the compound.

The Professor's voice was still echoing through the society, "All of you are incomplete — you are half men and the one you call Addha, see how complete he is, how perfect."

das paise aur dadi

A fight over a mere ten paise with his grandmother, and Chakku ran away from home. Ten paise is hardly anything. Ram Manohar's pockets are always jingling with money. He could buy a kite anytime he liked. The moment one of his kites was lost, he began to tie *kanni* in the next. His reel was always loaded with *manjha* and there was a stock of *saddi* in his house. He felt angry at the memory of all these things. Dadi is so secretive and spiteful! No wonder her face is covered with wrinkles! Ram's grandmother has no wrinkles at all. He was reminded of all of Dadi's defects. She has such loose ears! Whenever she kisses him on the cheeks her ears come swinging down on his eyes. And she has no eye lashes at all. Her eyes remain half-open when she sleeps and so does her mouth.

Drawing caricatures of Dadi in his imagination, he walked barefoot till he reached the railway station. He entered the station building aimlessly but the moment the guard blew his whistle, he ran and boarded the train waiting on the platform.

He thought of running away from home only after the train started moving. And right there in the moving train he decided that it was necessary to be self-sufficient and independent in life. This was no life where you had to beg such decrepit old people for a kite! No wonder his elder brother left Dadi to go and live in Bombay and has not come back for several years.

He fell asleep sitting at the door of the compartment. When he woke up after a long time it had grown dark outside. It occurred to him, for the first time, then, that he had really run away from home. He was less angry with Dadi now, but his complaints and grievances were still present like a lump in his throat.

Ten paise is not such a big deal and he had not stolen it. Taking ten paise from the *puja* bowl is not stealing because he had picked it up right in front of Bhagwan's eyes. Dadi herself says that her gods are ever awake.

"Do they stay awake day and night? Don't they ever sleep?"

She had answered, "Yes, they can see even with their eyes closed."

Hm. How come they did not see those ten paise? And if they did, why didn't they tell Dadi? She thinks that I have stolen money. Dadi's gods are sly, exactly like her. They are hard of hearing and have poor vision.

Someone asked him to leave the door and sit inside the compartment. May be they were approaching a station. The train was slowing down. By the time it came to a halt the thought of going back struck him once. However, he was scared out of his wits to see a policeman strolling on the platform. He also realized for the first time that he was ticketless. He had heard that people who travel without a ticket are arrested and sent to jail where they have to undergo rigorous imprisonment.

It had grown chilly near the door of the compartment. He moved inside and sat down between the berths. After the train started moving and passengers returned to their seats, he crawled up and down through piles of trunks, crates and bedrolls and settled right under a window.

He was now tormented by hunger. Also thirst. He noticed the water container belonging to the gentleman sleeping on an upper berth swaying with the movement of the train. And the glass placed upside down on its mouth was rattling continuously.

At the same time he saw the ticket checker in a blue uniform and wearing a shiny brass badge entering the compartment. Following him was his assistant holding a ticketless traveller by the scruff of his neck. Chakku was petrified. How come this man had entered a moving train? He had not seen him boarding the train at the station. He was sure those people had sat hiding somewhere before.

Crawling under the seat he somehow managed to reach behind the blue uniform. He crept to the other side of the compartment from where he could see the toilet. He went in quickly, shut the door and unfastening his knickers, sat on the toilet bowl. He felt safe. Who would come to ask for a ticket in the latrine, he thought. He also wondered why others did not use that trick. At least that man with a pockmarked face who was held by the scruff of his neck could have thought of it. He sat on the commode for quiet long. He could feel the cold air on his bare legs. After a while he started feeling sleepy.

Suddenly the train changed tracks. It gave him a jolt. The train began slowing down. He opened the door of the toilet cautiously and peered out. They were nearing some station. He looked around but found no evidence of the presence of the blue uniform. Chakku was convinced that the ticket checker was hiding somewhere. After all where could he go from a moving train? Chakku got off the train the moment it came to a halt.

It was a deserted station and the time was midnight. No one except Chakku had got off the train. The train stood panting for a while and then chugged off on its journey.

Chakku went to a bench and sat down shrinking with his head on his knees. Almost immediately he rolled off to one side like a pillow. A watchman with a lantern came knocking the ground with his staff and made him get up by boxing his ears.

"Get out of here. Have you run away from home? Run off otherwise the police will arrest you and put you to hard labour in the jail!"

Just one threat was enough to make him stagger. He stood up and the watchman disappeared knocking the ground with his staff. Chakku walked towards the lower side of the platform where he could see a pile of gunny sacks in the dim light. Behind the pile an old woman was sleeping with her mouth open like his Dadi. She was covered with a worn out quilt. She must be a beggar, he thought. By now he was completely overpowered by sleep. He crept into the sleeping woman's quilt feeling as if he was creeping into Dadi's quilt. Back in the village, the *mirasan* often made him sleep in her bed but he would get up in the middle of the night and creep into Dadi's quilt. Chakku fell asleep the moment his head touched the ground.

In the morning he woke up to discover that he had been sleeping nestling close to the old woman.

He saw some coins lying in a brass bowl near the beggar-woman's head. He was reminded of the *puja* bowl from which he had taken ten paise. He also felt extremely hungry for he had not eaten since the day before. He wondered what the old woman would do with so much loose change. Once he had asked Dadi why old people needed money and she had answered, "One needs money even after death. Otherwise who would cremate this body?"

"Liar!" Chakku had thought. There was such a lot of split wood in the house!

He looked at the brass bowl again. Would it matter if I take ten paise from here? There was no Bhagwan and no Dadi there. "May be I should ask her for the money. She may give it to me herself." He told himself. He looked around. He could see the smoke rising from the *angeethi* placed near the canteen swirling above the mist. He picked up a ten paise coin, adjusted the sleeping old woman's quilt over her and went towards the urinals. On coming out he washed his hands with some soil. Dadi had taught him that he should wash his hands with the ash from the *chulha* if he could not get soap.

"And what should I do if there is no ash?" he had queried.

"Then you should take a little earth from a flower pot but you should always wash your hands after visiting the urinal," she had answered.

He washed his hands with cold water. Someone had left powdered coal on the rim of the small tank around the water tap after cleaning his teeth. Chakku helped himself to the coal and cleaned his teeth with it. After that he washed his hands and face, shook his hands dry and when he put his hands in the pockets of his shorts his hand was stung by the cold ten paise coin.

When he returned to the platform he noticed three or four men standing near the old woman. One man sitting close to her head was saying, "She has gone absolutely stiff. She must have been dead now for eight to ten hours."

"She must have died in her sleep at night."

Chakku stopped short in his tracks. Some people were coming in that direction from the waiting room.

"What would become of her?"

"After the station master comes he would send the information."

"To whom?"

"To the municipality. Men from the municipality would take her away and cremate her."

The man sitting close to her pulled the quilt and covered her face with it. Chakku took out the ten paise coin from his pocket and flung it in the old woman's brass bowl.

Everybody looked at him but he shot off from that place. He ran fast. To go back to his Dadi.

ȘEEΜ∂

For the third time since that morning, the key to her former
house — Sudhir's house — had fallen into her hand as she
took out something from her purse. It was a year or more
since she had left Sudhir and yet every time she touched that
key while rummaging through the contents of her handbag,
she felt like telling the taxi driver, "Not this way. Please turn
in the opposite direction. I have just changed my husband."
She had really changed husbands rather in a desultory manner; just like that, in passing, like someone changing taxis on
the road.

A year had passed, still she did not feel that she had
left Sudhir. T.K. loves her and he is such an extrovert, and
a cheerful person. He came up with new antics and
surprises every day. One evening he came home suddenly in

a new car and said, "Come, let me teach you driving. I am
not going to keep a driver and I don't like you going around
in taxis. From today you have your own car and I have mine!"

However, she still travelled by taxis. Every time she took
the car out she would bang it somewhere or the other. She
just could not handle driving.

Just a few days before they had got married she had
mentioned how much she loved the sea and T.K. had gone
ahead and bought a bungalow by the sea. He had asked her
to sit in the car saying, "Come, let me give you a surprise."
He showed the bungalow to her and said, "This is my wedding gift to you!"

With T.K. it was like being continuously swept off one's
feet. Sudhir, on the other hand, kept her feet firmly planted
on the ground. It was always discipline, dedication.

The first thing to do in the morning was to gargle with
warm, saline water. It is the first exercise for clearing your
throat and voice for the theater. Reach the theater on time,
and write all your dialogues in your own hand. Memorize
them. He used to put her through rehearsals till she was bored
to tears. Stage movements were determined even to the extent
of drawing in and releasing your breath. Actors and actresses
would begin to resemble the properties on the stage and yet
no one dared to protest in front of Sudhir. He would explain
all nuances of method acting to his players, and yet manage
to display amazing spontaneity during the performance of the
play. An enthralled audience would always rise to its feet as
his plays drew to a close.

She was, nevertheless, bored with his theater. It made her
feel as if she was married to a Head Master and lived in a

classroom instead of a house.

One day she had asked lightly, "Do you think I should cut my hair? This length, see," she had gathered her long hair in her hands and turned it in at her shoulders to show him.

Sudhir had smiled and said calmly, "But what would become of Leela Beenare in *Adalat Jari Hai* if you do? And how about *Adhe Adhure?*"

She had become irritated. "You always visualize me through the characters in your plays. Have you ever looked at me as I am?"

Sudhir had tried to laugh it away but she remained unmoved. "I know if you have to choose between me and the theater, you'll choose theater. My place in your life is secondary and I do not like it at all."

Sudhir had smiled as usual, touched her chin and said, "Seema, my love, if I were to ask this question of myself even then I would choose the theater first, followed by you and then myself."

She had no answer to that but she did not like it at all.

She had never doubted Sudhir's affection and integrity but she had often wondered whether what he said amounted to a dialogue from a play. That was his style. He never raised his voice, was never stubborn and never lost his temper. There were no highs and lows in their domestic life. She wondered why the man who generated so much excitement with his presentation of dramatic ups and downs on stage was such a bore in his personal life. He was so bland. All that mattered to him was theater, just theater.

Once, only once he had expressed a wish to have a child

but she had excused herself saying, "I am scared of being pregnant."

"In that case, let me become pregnant!" He had laughed it away at that time but after a few days, perhaps on the day she had mentioned cutting her hair, he had said stuffing his papers in his bag, "Do you know what your problem is? Your problem is that you are scared of belonging — you don't wish to put shackles on your feet. You don't want to make a long term commitment. You wish to keep your options open all the time so that you could change tracks according to your whims. Remember, when we met you used to go to a painting school. Then you quit it to go to Pandit Giri Prasad to learn singing. Your tanpura went to rust but....."

Suddenly he had come and stood behind her and asked, "What are you doing?"

She was sitting in front of the mirror and drawing a moustache on her face with an eyebrow pencil. She had answered with a smile, "I want to see how I look with a moustache. How do I look? What if I was a man?"

Sudhir had resumed his analytical tune, "May be that is what your problem is." He had left swinging his bag.

"Very dramatic! Hunh!" She had snorted in irritation. "Is it always necessary to give the right answer? One should experience everything. I had not drawn this moustache for a serious analysis. It is quite possible to answer a joke with a joke. You don't have to pontificate on everything!"

She was itching to hurt Sudhir. That night she sat before the mirror for a long time and got up only when she heard the telephone bell ring. "Hello," she said. It turned out to be a wrong number. She answered, "No, it is not Susheela.

But could you manage with something less than Susheela? May be Sheela!"

The man on the other end flung an expletive at her. Seema laughed and replaced the receiver on the cradle. The mists cleared from her mind. In the meantime Mundu, the servant boy from her neighbour's house had come to take back his *ghia-ghas*. Seema asked him, "What is a *ghia-ghas?*

"You grate vegetables on it," he had answered.

"What will you do with it?"

"I'll grate *ghia* on it," he had answered. For a moment she was tempted to fling the expletive she had heard over the phone on the boy's face but she restrained herself from doing so. After he left she took off her clothes, threw them carelessly around and marched to the bathroom in the altogethers.

She was in for a scolding at the theater that day. Three pages were found missing from the script file.

"Where have they gone?"

"I have no idea."

"What do you mean you have no idea?"

"I don't know."

Sudhir's voice bounced like a ball, hit the ceiling and fell on her ears, "If you don't know, who should? You or I?" He thrust the script angrily in her hands and said again, "This is not your house. It is the theater. You can run a house without groceries but a theater can not be managed without a script."

She had deliberately gone for a movie alone from the theater. She had thought of taking Rukhsana with her but Rukhsana's behaviour was too girlish and she played up to Sudhir all the time. She wanted to ask Farrukh to come with her but Sudhir sent him off on some errand regarding the production. In the end she went by herself to a late show.

She had no hopes of finding Sudhir awake on her return. It was just as well that they had their own keys to the flat. After letting herself in, she noticed packets of Chinese food lying on the table. Looked like Sudhir had not eaten. She could hear a tape playing inside, a *ghazal* by Ghulam Ali. She knew Sudhir would have fallen asleep listening to it. She picked up the food and put it in the refrigerator, placed the script file on the shelf, turned off the tape recorder, switched off the light and went out on the balcony where she lay down on the cool floor. The sea was far but she could hear its rumbling.

It was almost two months since the kitchen tap had started leaking. You could hear it dripping, *tip trup,* day and night. Both Sudhir and she had mentioned it several times but neither of them had called a plumber. Seema was of the opinion that every husband ought to have a few basic skills such as driving a nail in the wall, mending a fuse, changing electric bulbs, unscrewing the bottles of medicines and blowing the corks just as he expects his wife to know how to cook and how to sew a button. She expected that Sudhir would fix that tap some day after he came home in the evening. But that was not to be.

One evening she tried her own hand at it, but flooded the kitchen as a result. There was no washer at home. Sudhir tried to stop the flow wrapping a strip of cloth around the tap. Seema came forward to lend him a hand in his efforts but she got carried away by the surging flow. She was drenched to the skin. If she let go of the tap the water would rise up to the ceiling. Both of them were still trying to contain the gushing water when Sudhir's old friend from college days, T.K., arrived suddenly. He was informal, well spoken and had a good sense of humour. He also turned out to be an accomplished plumber. He too got soaking wet in the process but he plugged the tap in two minutes flat. Sudhir had quite forgotten that he had invited T.K. to dinner that evening. Seema got quite flustered at this sudden revelation.

T.K. was an extremely informal person. He said, "Don't worry, Seema. I'd be perfectly happy if you feed me on an onion broken with a fist like Punjabis do!"

Sudhir chipped in, "We have neither an onion nor a Punjabi in the house! We'll have to send for both!"

T.K. solved that problem, too. He was quite a good cook. He stirred up something to eat in an hour's time. Seema had asked him, "What are your other accomplishments?"

"I don't know how to sing but I can play a transistor."

Dressed in Sudhir's clothes, T.K. looked like another version of Sudhir. They spent a cheerful evening tempered with lighthearted banter and jokes. She did not remember having laughed so much in that house before. Later she had said to Sudhir, "He is so relaxed and informal, this friend of yours! I have never seen anyone joking with you like that before. In the theater everybody behaves like a subordinate to you!"

Sudhir had looked up from the book he was reading. She had smiled and said, "Even I do," and turned over to the other side.

When T.K. came to return Sudhir's clothes he extended an invitation to them to come to his house. Sudhir was extremely preoccupied with his new production. *Adhe Adhure* was going to be staged. He had told Seema, "You can go directly to his house. I'll come there from the theater."

She had already said 'cheers' over champagne with T.K. before Sudhir reached the place. T.K. had kept her in splits that day too. Sudhir had arrived late and T.K. had joked, "You should take care of your wife, Sudhir. Otherwise she'll run away!"

"She can go wherever she wants provided she takes me with her!"

They had just been joking and it turned out to be true! Seema had quit the theater midway through the reading of *Adhe Adhure*. It was a similar fight in front of others as before. Sudhir was reading a few lines from the play.

"And then Jagmohan appeared on the scene. Contacts at high places, extravagant lifestyle, impeccable grooming and attractive manners — and you thought how lovely it would be had he been in Mahendra's place. The fact is that you would have the same thoughts about any man other than Mahendra, and you would have been convinced that you were married to the wrong man because for you the only meaningful life is the one in which you can grab, possess and surround yourself with as much as you can!"

This passage was followed by two or three lines of her dialogue. She had to be nudged to be reminded of her cue. 'I do not know why my attention was concentrated on T.K. I was feeling that Sudhir was taunting me by alluding to T.K. in the name of Jagmohan.' However, what he was saying was a part of the script. She had read that play by Mohan Rakesh earlier, too, much before she had met T.K. Her timing deteriorated steadily as the rehearsals got underway. One day

Sudhir just exploded in front of everybody. She also gave it back to him.

"Don't scream at me in front of others. I'm not just an artiste working for you. I am also your wife."

"You may be my wife at home. Here you are an artiste like all others."

"I can't be mute as a cow like others who look at you as if you are not a director but God incarnate!"

Sudhir looked at her in astonishment at that last sentence. She had flung the file away and continued, "I am not going to do this play. I am fed up of your theater!"

Sudhir's voice had gone considerably lower when he said, "At home you are bored with the house and here you are fed up of the theater. You always want to be at a place other than where you are. You are never satisfied with what you have. You yourself do not know where you are and where you want to be."

And an amazing thing happen that day. Sudhir left the theater and went away.

They did not talk to each other for weeks after this incident. At least about the theater there was no talk at all.

In the beginning she used to call T.K. Then he started telephoning her. He would pick her up from home and drop her back. They did not realize when and why they started keeping their meetings secret from Sudhir. She knew Sudhir was not suspicious by nature but what would he say if he saw her in T.K.'s arms? Won't he ask anything if he saw her leaving T.K.'s house?

If he confronted her she would definitely be upset. "Do you suspect me?" And if he did not ask anything she would be equally upset. "Are you so indifferent to me?"

T.K.'s arm was clasped around her waist as she inserted the key in the front door. She pushed open the door and they stepped in together only to find Sudhir standing right there. They were taken aback. Sudhir's face was expressionless. T.K. desperately tried to remain normal. He asked Sudhir, "What are you up to these days? Which play are you involved with?"

"I have become entangled in a somewhat personal drama."

"Meaning?"

"Meaning that..... Sit down, Seema."

She was nervous. Sudhir resumed speaking, "Actually it is someone else's show. I have been caught in it for no apparent reason."

"Meaning?"

"Meaning that ..... There is a certain Mr. Mukherji with us at the theater."

"Mukherji? Who?" she had asked.

"May be you don't remember him. God knows if there is anything worth remembering in him but people remember him because he has a beautiful wife. She is both beautiful and talented. What has happened is that someone has fallen in love with her. You can say that she has fallen in love with someone."

T.K. and Seema exchanged glances, Sudhir went on as if he was explaining a situation in a play to them. "And love is such a wretched thing. It can pull the carpet from under the feet of the steadiest persons and they begin to believe that it is the only thing worth aspiring for in life. Other things — art, talent, are mere fripperies. It is well and good if you possess them and it does not matter if you don't."

"Pontificating again — the same analysis ... she interrupted him, "So, what is Mukherji's problem?"

"His problem is that he has come to know of the affair and he wants to know what he should do. Should he stay quiet and let things run their natural course or leave his wife? Should he throw her out? What should he do?"

Sudhir's voice had started getting hoarse gradually. Both T.K. and Seema understood what he was saying. One of the *dramatis personae* rose to leave but Sudhir spoke to him in a cold, harsh tone, "Sit down, T.K. You are not a child. You do understand what I am saying." He went on, "Look there is no such thing as a lawful husband or a lawful wife. These legal stamps are clamped on these relationships unnecessarily. You can get ration cards made with such stamps but they are quite useless in forging relationships."

Seema had noticed anger and resentment in Sudhir's voice for the first time. He was saying in a restrained voice. "To date no one has been able to prevent the inevitable. You cannot stop what has to happen. And I refuse to go on with this cancer in my life. If the two of you are not playing the fool and if you genuinely love each other, take each other's hand and get out of this house. Get lost!"

Sudhir had burst into tears. How she longed to get up and hold him but the telephone bell had rung at the same time and Sudhir had kicked the instrument in anger. She could hear a voice whimpering "hello, hello" in the receiver lying on the floor. Sudhir had moved forward and stood there holding the front door open for them to leave. His voice had grown hoarse, "I want to have your decision. Now..... This moment."

She had cut her hair immediately after her marriage to T.K. In effect, she had chopped off the hair of Leela Beenare and Savitri. She wanted to forget the theater but she could not forget Sudhir. T.K. had taken her to Cochin where his fishing trawlers operated. It was an altogether new experience to live on the sea for eight to ten days. T.K. would tease her, "Living on the sea, you have grown more *namkin!*"

Noticing tears in her eyes one day, he had sat by her. Cupping her face in his hands, he had said, "Do I see Sudhir's face in these tears?"

"Hmm," she had nodded in affirmation.

"It is easy to break a relationship after a fight and a tussle. You can snap the ties and forget the other person. But Sudhir has bound us forever by loosening his hold like this. I am guilty for this whole episode."

T.K.'s love was genuine. There was no artificiality in it.

An unusual thing had happened soon after they returned from Cochin. She heard the sound of gargling early one morning. Jumping out of bed, she went to the bathroom and found T.K. gargling at the wash basin.

"What are you doing?"

"I am gargling. I have a sore throat."

She poured the warm saline water in the wash basin and said, "There is no need to gargle. Come, I'll send for some medicines for you."

She called up her doctor immediately but he was unavailable. T.K. left for office. In the evening she went to the doctor's clinic. The moment he saw her, the doctor said, "I did go to see him. I have examined Sudhir. It is the same chronic problem with his tonsils."

Seema had stopped short in her tracks. She had forgotten to tell the doctor she did not stay in that house anymore. Looked like Sudhir hadn't told him either.

"In my opinion he needs surgery to remove his tonsils, but he does not listen to me. He said he'll talk to you and then get back to me and agreed to have the operation if you pressed hard for it."

She knew that Sudhir would never agree for surgery. He would suffer the pain but would do nothing about his tonsils. He was a real coward in such things. She remembered what an uproar was created when his tonsils were to be painted with glycerine. She had to sit on his chest pinning down both his arms with her legs and warning him, "Please co-operate and let me apply it properly, otherwise I'll pour the entire bottleful down your throat! Open your mouth, now open.....!"

The taxi came to a halt at her bungalow. As she reached for money in her purse to pay the taxi driver, she touched the old key again. The watchman opened the door of the taxi and informed her, "There was a call from Saheb from Cochin. He won't be coming today. He said he'll call up at night."

Suddenly her mind was crowded with a lot of apprehensions. What would Sudhir think? How would he meet her? She had heard only the other day that he was unwell. She had seen him only once during the last one year or more when she had got off a taxi and Sudhir had come forward to hire it. She had a hundred rupee note. The taxi driver was about to start grumbling about change when Sudhir had shut him up. He had told her that he would pay on her behalf and that she should move on. After that he had got into the taxi and left.

After that incident, her taxi had stopped near Sudhir's building once again today.

Taking the lift, she went up to his floor. She stood in front of the door for a while. She pressed her ear on the door once but heard no sound. May be he was not at home.

Suddenly the neighbour's door opened and Mundu, the servant boy breezed past her with a hasty "Namaste, Memsaheb," and ran down the stairs.

The lift was still waiting on that floor. Taking all her courage in her hands, she turned the key in the door lock, opened the door quietly and entered the flat. She stopped and stood there, hesitant. Things looked exactly the same as before except that there was an air of disarray in the room. She was in the process of picking up a cushion that had fallen on the floor when she heard the sound of girlish laughter coming from Sudhir's room. The girl was saying, "Please let me apply it properly — just let me put this medicine on your tonsils. Come — get it done properly otherwise....."

That was followed by the sound of Sudhir's coughing and the girl's laughter.

Seema turned on her heels swiftly, closed the door behind her and dashed into the lift. The lift moved downwards and then it struck her that she had left the key in the door lock! At last it had reached where it belonged! Just as well. It would no longer rub against her hand when she put it in her purse!

satranga

A number of people screwed up their noses, scratched the napes of their necks and turned over in their beds as the echoes of Khairu's song floated towards their houses from the *chaupal* in the middle of the night.

"Oof Oh! This bloke has no work in the day and no rest at night!"

Mamdu's wife was still awake but she said in a sleepy voice, "The wretched man does not take up any occupation!" Both husband and wife turned over and fell asleep again. At the *chaupal* Khairu lay alone singing deep into the night.

Everybody in that village was dreadfully busy. Nobody ever seemed to take a break. He was the only one without work. He slept at the *chaupal* and waking up very early in the morning, made his way to the waterwheel. After hanging his bag by the stump of a tree he would take off his clothes, wash them and hang them up to dry. Then he would take a long bath which ended only when his clothes were dry and easy to wear again.

He had no home and hearth. Where could he go? So he sauntered towards Mamdu's fields. But Mamdu was preoccupied with work and paid no attention to him. All through the day he sweated out ploughing his fields, mending the earthen fences or crushing clumps of earth. Taking out his flute from his bag Khairu would stand on the plough next to Mamdu or start narrating a dream he had the previous night. Mamdu did not know how to react to him. He could neither ask him to stop nor quit the place himself. On one occasion when Khairu stopped the plough so that he could paint the horns of the bullocks, Mamdu was really angry. He said, "Get off! I have no time for your stupid whims!"

Khairu drew back at that time but in the afternoon when Mamdu was having his lunch, he quickly went and painted the bullocks horns'. Mamdu's wife went on calling him to come and eat but he remained absorbed in what he was doing.

Najjo was saying to Mamdu, "Please finish your lunch quickly. I have to go back and feed Sameena."

Mamdu instructed her to give medicine to Taju. She said again, "I'll go and fill the water vessels while you eat."

"Didn't you fill them in the morning?"

"No, I couldn't. I had gone to the mill to get the wheat ground," she answered.

"Please get the quilts stuffed at Bush *Chacha's*," he reminded her.

"I still have to sift the paddy," she said. Khairu considered all these chores useless. However, everyone else was busy, very busy doing them.

It was the same story the next day. As Mamdu started his lunch he called out to Khairu. Khairu was busily taking out some brass bells from his bag and stringing them.

"Khairu, what are you doing?"

"I'm putting these bells around the necks of the bullocks. It'll be so nice to hear them tinkle when they move," Khairu answered.

"Come now — come and eat. Let go of these idle pursuits. Bells or no bells, the bullocks will go on. That is their job."

"You too are like the bullocks," Khairu joked, "Why don't you wear one of the bells?"

In the evening, Khairu arrived at the well. He was quite thirsty but no one had time to offer him water. Everybody looked dreadfully busy. One had to rush back and season the *dal* and the other had already prepared the dough for the *rotis*. The third one was anxious about her mother who was ill. The fourth was rubbing her brass pitcher with a sliced lemon. Two or three of them were drawing water together. Khairu sat down on one side. He took out a few colours from his bag and started drawing patterns on an earthen pitcher.

"Khairu —"

The girl turned round and looked at him but she could not retrieve her pitcher from him. Everything Khairu did was useless. Still, even those who protested did not stop him and those who felt sorry for him would just say 'poor thing' and keep quiet. However, nothing in the village was ever stalled because of his presence. As soon as her turn to draw water came, the girl picked up her pitcher from Khairu's lap. By now Khairu had become an expert. He had kept carving a niche for himself during such little gaps between people's preoccupations.

On one occasion he had stopped at Heera the weaver's house. Heera was weaving a *khes*. Khairu stood watching him at work as he listened to the rhythm of the warp. The whole day he hummed the same rhythm around the village.

"Dhutang-tung! Dhutang-tung! Dhutang-tung!"

That day, the *Mukhiya* declared that Khairu had gone out of his mind.

The next day Khairu visited Heera again.

"Heera *chacha*, why do you weave with thread in just one colour? Why don't you mix and match the yarn in two or three colours?"

"I do it because I have still not lost my mind," Heera snapped.

"But *chacha*, that would look prettier," he said.

"A *khes* is meant for spreading on a cot and not to look at," was the curt reply.

How could poor Khairu convince him? Heera's daughter Barkha happened to be standing with a basket full of cotton yarn right there. She burst out laughing at Khairu's discomfiture. As she placed the basket near the loom her hair came undone and tumbled down her shoulders. And while she went in rearranging it in a knot, Khairu felt inexplicably abashed.

"Barkha," He called her clearly by her name. She turned round and stood waiting.

"Will you let me have some yarn?" He asked.

"What'd you do with it?"

"I'll make a *parandi* for you," the shy Khairu answered

brazenly, "But don't give me just one colour. Let me have the yarn in all colours."

The poor man had to make several trips to obtain and collect all those colours. The day he had accumulated them all, he settled down under the big banyan tree and started making a *parandi* singing "Dhutang tung-Dhutang-tung".

People laughed as they went past him. Only the school master stopped by and asked, "What are you doing, Khairu?"

He kept quiet for a moment, then answered laughing, "I am weaving a *parandi* for thick, dark clouds!"

It is a fact that no one had ever seen him working. But on the other hand no one could say that he was totally idle.

He roamed the village several times between the waterwheel in the morning and the *chaupal* at night. He would cross a house thousands of times but suddenly one day he would stop at its door. Then, producing a knife from his bag he would scratch a drawing on the door. In this way he had carved the figures of peacocks and deers and the signs of *Swastika* on several doors. He had no belongings except his bag but he strode through the village as if he was the lord of all he surveyed. He stopped where he liked and moved ahead when he wished. He sat by whoever tolerated him and moved off if someone told him to go. He accepted what people gave him and gave whatever he could when it was asked for. It was a journey into a great distance and still it was a journey to nowhere.

And in the middle of the night when all were asleep, his voice would rise forth to wake them up. They would screw up their noses, shake their quilts and turn over to the other side.

It was inevitable that people would lose their patience with him. How long could they go on feeding him and providing him with clothes for winter and summer?

Then Khairu started keeping poor health. However, he hid his sorrows in his usual colours, bearing his hardships silently.

And one day the *Mukhiya* got up in the middle of the night, and came to the *chaupal*.

"You good for nothing parasite!" he thundered. Poor Khairu fell down after just one slap.

The few windows which were open were quickly closed.

That morning nearly everyone passed by the *chaupal*. Khairu was nowhere to be seen. His bag was hanging there as usual. People asked each other about his whereabouts to no avail. He was not seen even at the waterwheel. Nor in the fields. Nor at the well.

For the first time people became aware of the peacocks carved on their doors. For the first time Mamdu stopped his bullock and touched the bells around their necks. Someone sighed at the well before picking up her small pitcher. Work which had never come to a standstill, paused and waited at every step — it was as if Khairu's name had risen from their lips to reflect in their eyes.

It was past midnight. A forsaken bag hung alone at the *chaupal* — and ... the entire village lay wide awake even without the echoes of that voice.

babu ki aag

Fire is not a plaything. It bites and claws and tears the flesh. Fire is a beast and it is rather strange that, at the same time, it is a bird and an insect, too; an insect like a wasp, small and yellow, which leaves a blister when it stings.

About 15 lakh years ago when people lived in tribes, they climbed trees and slept on their boughs to protect themselves from wild animals. They spent their lives hiding in the caves. There was little difference between man and beast at that time. Man hunted animals and animals hunted human beings. Survival of the fittest was the rule of the jungle. Both animals and human beings roamed the forests in large groups.

There was a young boy in a tribe whose thoughts ran as follows. Why does night fall? Where does the sun go? His house must be on the other side of the hills. But if it is so how come he reappears in the morning from the opposite direction?

That boy was called Habu. He used to think that the sun went to the ocean for a bath but wondered which route he took. He was convinced that the sun went stealthily because he had to go naked. Habu thought he would definitely go and meet the sun once he found out what he was all about. He also intended to take an animal skin with which the sun could cover himself.

He thought and thought till he was exhausted. Thousands of questions swirled around in his mind. He could not even remember them all.

Sometime he would wonder why babies were born to women and not to men. How he wished to give birth to a baby! He also thought that he would not be scared of any wild animal if he could fly. When chased by one, he would just go and sit on the back of an elephant like a crow. One day he climbed a tree and tried to fly from there but he fell down with a thud. What is more Bakha kicked him for doing such a silly thing. Everybody laughed at his injuries. Only his mother felt his pain.

It rained hard one night. Jumbi asked Habu, "Where does so much water come from?"

Habu had a ready answer to the question, "A tribe of gods live in the sky. It rains on earth when they go to urinate collectively."

Jumbi was astonished to hear such a clever answer. He said admiringly, "Habu, you too would become the head of the tribe like Bakha one day. You have a stomach full of knowledge!" Actually he meant to say that Habu was extremely intelligent but at that time the stomach was considered to be the seat of intellect.

Habu's learning grew with his age. In time he started searching for answers for the questions which were raised in his mind. People were astonished when he talked about things he had learned or known. Even Bakha was amazed at times.

Habu was the one who revealed the mystery behind the thundering of the clouds. "When gods fight among themselves, a lot of their bones get broken. Thunder is the noise made by the crackling of those bones." Ever since he had started finding answers his influence had grown in the tribe.

Habu had often seen crows perched on an elephant's back. They were not disturbed either by the flapping of the elephant's ears or the flicking of his little tail. He had often seen an elephant passing by alone. The elephant went to the beach every day where he frolicked in water and then lay on the sand. Habu had long wished to move above ground. One day he took all his courage in his hands and sat on a tree waiting for the elephant. As soon as the elephant came under the tree, Habu jumped and landed on his back. It was an entirely new experience for the elephant so he was unnerved a bit. First he went in circles, then trumpeted loud and shook his tail but when nothing worked he ran towards the jungle. Habu was delighted. When the elephant was passing under a tree, he sprang up, caught hold of a branch of the tree and escaped.

Habu did it again after two or three days. The elephant trumpeted and ran but Habu had his ride and made his escape like before. One day the elephant caught Habu and his friends bathing in the sea. He drew in a lot of water in his trunk and sprayed it on Habu's face. All the others ran away in terror but the elephant wrapped Habu in his trunk, lifted him up and placed him on his back. Before he could recover his wits and jump off, the elephant moved into deeper waters. Habu screamed again and again but the elephant kept throwing water on him with his trunk. The elephant enjoyed himself thoroughly. After a while Habu stopped screaming. At length he realized that the elephant was not fighting but playing with him. Arriving at the beach, Habu's tribesmen were astonished to see Habu and the elephant playing like friends. That had never happened before. A fearsome wild animal had been tamed by Habu. All were awe inspired by the spectacle. And the day Habu came towards his tribe sitting on the back of the elephant, they were wonderstruck. However, they were no longer scared of the animal now. They went close to him and offered him something to eat which the elephant received with his trunk and devoured cheerfully. From then on the elephant became a part of their tribe.

Human beings could experience the heat and the cold but they did not know why they felt hot and why their bodies shivered with cold. They had found dens and lairs to protect themselves from rain but they were not aware of the cycle of the seasons till then. They had not yet learned to measure time. They were conscious of the difference between night and day but were totally ignorant about months or years. Naturally they did not know how long a season lasted and that it returned every year. The rain and the sun had been parts of their lives as they are of ours but there were no books at that time and learning was passed through word of mouth from generation to generation.

During winter one year there was a stupendous flash of lightning. Habu had seen lightning before and was aware that when it flashed it lighted up vast distances. You could see everything as clearly as during the day time. But that year there was ear-splitting thunder, and lightning that seemed to descend on the forest. At a short distance you could see a strange animal sitting on a dried up tree and devouring it. As the branches of the tree split and fell, the animal gradually moved down the tree. The body of the animal sent out light like the sun. You could see everything clearly in that light. People from Habu's tribe ran and gathered around it. Such an animal had never been seen before, not even in the time of Bakha's forefathers.

It was fire.

It is not known when it acquired this name. It is also not known when it transformed from masculine to feminine gender. But at first it was considered a male animal.

That was an enormous tree. One or two smaller, dried up trees stood near it. As the flames leapt out towards them the people from the tribe would scream, "Look, look, he is going to catch the next tree." By the time the next tree was engulfed by the flames the shrinking animal grew huge again. The top of the first tree had disappeared completely. They were all agreed on one thing.

"He has devoured it. He has devoured it."

For the first time man had seen the animal who had eaten up a whole tree. That animal kept devouring the trees all night. Morning came but 'it' was still at it. Others ate their kill and left but that animal refused to leave. 'It' killed his prey and sat and ate the trees right there. There were more trees at a small distance. Habu thought that the animal had either not seen those trees or by then his hunger was satisfied. He asked Bakha who expressed a sensible opinion.

"I think this animal eats dried up trees. But it has never been seen in the jungle before," Bakha modified his opinion slightly.

"It must be a bird overflying the jungle and must have alighted on seeing a dried up tree." Habu conjectured.

"But 'it' had never been seen flying in the sky." Bakha modified his opinion a little more. "I think 'it' is some animal from the skies. 'It' had fallen from the abode of the gods. Don't you see it has the same colour as the gods?"

By now Bakha was convinced about his understanding. The others also agreed with him to some extent. Another thing at which Habu was bewildered was that the others grew fat after eating but that animal grew smaller in size in spite of eating so much. He had noticed that the place where the animal was sitting and eating had turned quite red.

In Jumbi's opinion 'it' had, like a lion, gone to sleep after eating. Tumba was a great one for daring. He declared, "I'll wake 'it' up if 'it' is sleeping."

He stretched out his hand to wake 'it' up by touching 'it' but recoiled with a scream. Fire had bitten him hard on his hand.

The feel of burning had never been experienced before that. The word 'burn' was created after 'fire'. Blisters had formed on Tumba's hand and people noticed that hairs had disappeared from his arm.

"He has licked them away," Tumbi said looking at the blisters.

"They must be the marks of 'its' teeth."

"You can't see any teeth."

"How could 'it' bite off the hairs, then?"

" 'It' did bite but no blood came out."

Tumba was still irritated. He plucked a long twig from a tree and started raking the fire with it. Everybody moved back cautiously. Fire remained unmoved for a while. You could see that the part of the twig thrust into 'its' belly was gradually turning black. Suddenly flames leapt from 'it' and a nervous Tumba tried to fling 'it' away. However, 'it' got caught in the animal skin tied around his waist. The moment the skin fell down, it started burning.

An uproar followed. Tumba stood naked before the crowd. In a moment fire ate up both the twig and the skin.

"This animal has grown big again!" Tumbi said, " 'It' eats up everything."

Two or three people threw huge rocks at 'it' and waited but fire could not eat them. Habu said, " 'It' does not have teeth so the rocks have turned black but he has not been able to crush them."

Habu gathered another thing and that was that fire had many mouths and could eat from several sides at a time. Another thing was that 'it' did not have feet so 'it' could not go to get food. 'It' ate as much as 'it' got. When the food finished 'it' began to die out, too.

Ever since he had adopted the elephant Habu was keen to also adopt a lion but after seeing fire he was tempted to adopt 'it'. When he saw the fire dying out he collected dry twigs from here and there and put them on fire. Fire grew big again.

At night he told his mother, The only way to keep fire alive is to keep feeding 'it'. 'It' dies if 'it' does not eat."

His mother asked, "What'll you do with fire?"

"See, there is light when the fire is around. You can see everything even at night and wild animals stay away from him. They run away scared. If we adopt fire no animal will attack our tribe."

It was a convincing argument. Bakha too nodded his head in affirmation. As a matter of fact nobody countered Habu anymore because he was so sensible.

The tribe gladly accepted Habu's proposal. Instead of hunting everyday they started collecting dry, broken twigs to feed that new animal. They longed to reach out and touch 'it' but every time they did that, fire bit them.

Habu was now talked about not only in his own tribe but also outside it. A number of other tribes also came to see fire. Then one day a dreadful accident took place.

It rained hard that day and Habu's entire tribe saw their red and gold animal dying a painful death. Seeing the rising smoke for the first time they thought that it was fire's life that must be ascending heavenwards. That convinced them even more that 'it' had come from the abode of gods in the sky. After a while all that remained was a heap of ashes which they considered to be the body of fire. Tumbi said a peculiar thing.

"It means that everybody's life goes upwards after death."

Habu queried, "But do you ever see it?"

Tumbi did know the answer to that but this question has remained in the mind of man since then. People still seek the answer to the question as to where man goes after his death.

jamun ka per

"Geo—r—gie," a shrill, high pitched voice rang through the street from one end to the other. Flora, George's mother was a middle-aged woman with a dark complexion but extremely fine facial features. "What do you mean leaving the house to play marbles so early in the morning? Come home, Papa is calling you."

"In a moment, Mummy. Let me finish this turn and I'll be right there," George shouted from across the street.

Babu from the house next door craned his neck and screwed his left eye in a pronounced wink. Flora smiled at him and went in.

Ahmed wiped the secretion from his eyes with his fingers. Selecting a *bunta*, he held it between his fingers, twisted his lips with deliberate affectation and tossed it in the air. The *bunta* fell very close to the pitch and the small marble scurried into the pitch like a frightened mouse. Ahmed won the game again. George took out the last marble from his pocket. Wiping it on his shorts, he looked at it longingly and handed it over to Ahmed.

"It does not matter, *beta*," eight year old George was telling Ahmed who was nine. "You are always a winner when we play *unti*. Just wait till you play *gutthi* with me."

"Is that so? Come play *gutthi* with me then!"

"I'll be back after Papa leaves for office." George ran across the street and disappeared into the staircase of his house. Sitting down with his back against the Jamun tree, Ahmed emptied the contents of his heavy pocket in the palm of his hand. He picked out the best marbles, popped them in his mouth one by one and after moistening them with saliva, polished them before storing them in a separate pouch. The gong in the clock-tower struck seven.

"Hurry up Amma. I am getting late for school."

"Here, son, take it." Amma put two paise worth of jaggery twists in Nikke's pocket.

"How come you have not returned my marble yet, Nikke?"

Frightened, Nikke stopped in his tracks. He looked at Amma for help.

"Let him go, boy. Please let him go to school." Amma said as she arranged her hawker's basket. Ahmed stepped forward and caught hold of Nikke's satchel.

"Why? Won't you behave yourself?" Amma stretched her arm towards Ahmed. Ahmed darted his hand into Nikke's pocket, grabbed a couple of jaggery twists and gobbled them up. By then Amma had held him by his shirt fronts saying, "I'll take you to Deenu, you rascal. Trust you to start bullying the children in the neighbourhood at the crack of dawn!"

"Let go of me, you old hag, otherwise I'll break your legs. Let go, or I'll reduce you to a pulp!" Ahmed yelled.

"Come, come, Deenu is the only one who can fix you."

"Deenu can do nothing to me. Let go of me or I'll topple your basket."

"Is this how you should speak about your father? Aren't you ashamed of yourself?" Amma slapped Ahmed on the nape of his neck. A number of marbles popped out of his pocket and rolled off the road.

"Decrepit old hag!" Ahmed shouted picking up the marbles and running away

"Bastard! I'll f—— your mother. Just come here, you wretch!" Standing outside his shop at the end of the road, Deenu, the blacksmith called out to his son.

Paltu saala was his special favourite among all abusive words. He started his day with a shower of abuses, its repertoire ranging between *saala* and bastard on the one hand and declaration of intentions to do unprintable things to his son's mother and sister, on the other. Deenu was about forty-five years of age but he had already developed a stoop. Thin and short of stature, this man nevertheless possessed tremendous energy. Dressed in a dirty *lungi* and khaki vest and with a cap of woven cane on his lead, he struggled against hot iron all day. At the end of the day when he finished his work and came to sit on the charpoy outside his shop, Mahmood prepared his *hookah* and placed it near him. Hanif and Akram pressed his legs before calling it a day. After resting for a while and enjoying a smoke, Deenu would blow his nose and wipe his hands on his *lungi*. Returning to the place, Mahmood would carry the charpoy and the *hookah* inside the shop, place them there and lock up. Finally Deenu would come home reciting, "*Al Hamdo-Rab-il-aalemin.*"

Deenu has been staying in the Fasih Building for over twenty years. In 1945 this building across the road from the Jamun tree had not yet been constructed. Basanti used to set up her flower shop under this same Jamun tree and Deenu used to work at fitting horse-shoes at the crossing of the same road. They were madly in love with each other. Every time the tall, blue-eyed Basanti passed through the crossing with her basket full of flowers, Deenu's biceps flexed and he delivered a sturdy blow of his hammer on the horse's hoof with the accompaniment of some choice expletive. Basanti would look at him with a smile and move on her way.

Subsequently Malik from the wholesale market married her in exchange for five hundred rupees paid to her father and brought her forcibly to his house. Nothing could stand up to Malik's money power. Both law and the impact of Deenu's hammer remained ineffectual against it. After coming to Fasih Building, Basanti had become the landlady and Deenu had grown from a horse-shoe maker into a full fledged blacksmith. He had established his shop on the same side of the road as Fasih Building.

Sardar Sohan Singh who conducted a money lending business from the same building lived on top of Deenu's shop. He had a lot of grievances against Deenu. One of them was that

Deenu started hammering at hot iron in his shop from early in the morning. That disturbed his sleep. Another was that Deenu had a loud voice in which he used a much abusive language. He had cribbed about Deenu to almost everybody in the building. However, he had not dared to go and speak directly to Deenu about his grievances.

"Tell me, who can really speak to him? What if he begins to abuse me?" Sardar Sohan Singh always concluded this topic with this sentence.

But on one occasion when Deenu called his son names, Sardar Sohan Singh flew into a rage. After he cooled down a bit, Deenu said politely, "Sardarji, which bastard has abused your son? How can this *paltu saala* (meaning himself) even scowl at your children? I consider them my own children, Sardarji." Helpless, Sardar Sohan Singh fell silent.

As the clock began to chime, Gajju looked over his shoulder at the clock tower. The time was 10 a.m. Putting his child's medicines in his pocket, he started walking faster. Seeing Sardarji standing outside his shop, he hesitated a bit and thought he would cross over to the other side but Sardarji had already noticed him. His pace slackened again.

"*Jai Ramji ki,*" Gajju came close with folded hands. Sardarji acknowledged his greeting by a slight nod.

"I haven't yet received your second instalment, Gajju," he said.

"I'll pay you next month, *huzoor*. My child has fallen ill ..."

"All right, pay me next month. But listen, take this charpoy to the Jamun tree and ask Mirzaji to come there. Tell him to bring the shatranj with him."

Gajju placed the charpoy under the Jamun tree and went to call Mirzaji.

"Come, play your card. This is the king of spades."

"Go on. I have put a mark at the back of that card and I know it is the Knave of Hearts."

Noora, Mohan, Babu and Kallan were playing cards sitting on the next charpoy. The afore mentioned card was a thin cardboard replacement for a torn card.

"These motifs are the symbols of spades, not of hearts."

"Do, you see the image of the King in this picture?"

"No I don't. I can see your image in it,"

"I can see your fathers'!" Mohan retaliated, enraged.

"It must be the image of that black sweeper woman of yours who beat you up with her broom!" Mohan said sarcastically. Noora flung the cards and moved away.

He muttered, "As if these blokes know how to play cards!"

"Go on. You are the one who does not know how to play!"

"Noora," Ahmed called out from the other side of the Jamun tree, "Shall we set up an *unti*?"

"Not an *unti*. But we can play *gutthi*."

"Okay. Let us play with three marbles each."

"Shall I play at a *paintra*?"

"That is what I'll do, too."

Kallan abandoned the cards and ran to join the boys on the other side of the tree. With one more player dropping out, the game of cards was suspended but Mohan went on shuffling the cards.

"Let us play *teen-do-paanch*," Chachchad suggested.

"It'll be more fun playing *chor* card," Babu commented.

"No, no. We'll play only colour. Some one or the other is bound to join us soon. I wonder why the boys haven't turned up yet. It is time Jogendra was here. He must be on his way. Look, Iqbal's there. Just ask him to come this way." Chachchad pointed at the postman moving towards the turning on the road. He waved at the postman who happened to be looking towards the Jamun tree. The postman waved back from a distance.

"Tell me what is going on, *Huzoor*?" he asked pleasantly.

"We were playing cards, *yaar*, but Kallan ditched us. Come, join us. Lets play a few hands."

"I'm afraid I can't. I still have to distribute letters from this bundle."

"Come on *yaar*, you can do it later. You don't exactly deliver the mail on time every day."

"No, no. I'll be thrown out of the postal department if somebody complains."

"Do come and sit down. Who'll complain today if no one has done it for three years." Mohan held Iqbal by the hand and forced him to sit on the charpoy.

"I must go. Please excuse me, *Huzoor*," Iqbal got up.

"I get it, *beta*. I am sure you have a letter to deliver at the house of your heart-throb!" Kallan mocked.

In the meanwhile, Mirza Saheb, who had tossed a pawn from the shatranj set on his hand, called out, "Do you have a letter for me?"

"I am afraid not, *Huzoor*. But I have one for Lalaji."

Lala Lekhraj, who was in the middle of explaining a move to Sardar Sohan Singh, stood up and said, "To hell with your *gora*. Take care, Mirza." Twirling his moustache, Sardar

Sohan Singh looked at Mirzaji and concentrated on the next move.

By the time the clock struck twelve the life under the Jamun tree had come alive to its full form. All day long there was a bustle under that tree but the busiest time was the afternoon. Returning from their schools, children rushed to play marbles and *langar* under the tree. Workers who returned from night shifts at 3 or 4 a.m. would, by then, be awake and engaged in the games of cards, shatranj or *chausar* after their lunch. Others from Fasih Building would be sitting and gossiping in the shade and older people would be discussing politics at a separate spot.

"Let it be Muslim League and not Congress if you will, but the real objective is independence," Vaidji said decisively.

"The main thing, Vaidji, is that we have to throw the *gora* (British) out first. Other things could be taken care of afterwards. After all we are all brothers. We can set the things amongst ourselves even if we quarrel." Jaichand had a way of explaining things in detail."

"Yes, of course. After all Hindus, Muslims and Sikhs are brothers," Sardar Sohan Singh asserted.

Lala Lekhraj listened to all these sentiments in silence. Very often he would even get up and go. He held an important position in the Ganesh Mills. He didn't say anything here but was often heard telling the workers at the mill, "If at all we get independence, it will be through Gandhiji and Gandhiji does not want to win freedom by antagonising the British. After all they are the rulers. They can have all those who talk against them eliminated, but they don't do that. Instead, they provide food, clothes and shelter to all. After all, what is wrong with them? They can have Jawaharlal and Gandhi murdered but they don't do it because they value good people." This political discourse revolved round two or three phrases which had more feelings than facts. After a while such discussion would take a different direction.

The respective shatranj armies of Sardar Sohan Singh and Mirzaji would engage in their conflict mounted on the charpoy in the cooling shade of the Jamun tree. Nehru would move along with the *vazir* and as the *ghoda* was moved Sardar Patel would fall in the orbit of Jinnah. Gandhiji was conspicuously absent from that shatranj because it was an aggressive war to eliminate the British rulers and non-violence could have no place in it. In spite of that, it included a large number of Gandhiji's followers who moved along with the *piadas* in slow measures.

The workers on night shift kept themselves occupied in the games of shatranj and *chausar* during the day. The card players concluded one round and shuffled the cards for the next to the drone of the flies which became audible during such intervals. One of them would comment, "Had you refrained from playing the six of spades, you'd have gained another victory." Another would add, "In fact it was your fault. You should have got rid of one colour in one go."

Such conversations were suddenly slashed by a loud comment rising from another assembly closeby, "*Dhut tere ki*! This *tissar* has fallen to my lot again!" It was Bishna talking to Diwan as he collected his *cowries*.

"It doesn't matter, *patthe*. Just you wait till I toss the dice next."

Nikka, Beera and Shoti would climb up the Jamun tree. They dangled their *langars* on the basket of the *paan* seller and chanted in shrill, high pitched voices, *"Laale ki chhabri par lai langar."* But Lala just sat indolently, nodding at his hawker's basket, Occasionally when the string was extra loose, the langar would strike against the bald pate of Lala who would startle and say, "Shall I prepare a Benarasi *paan*, ji?"

The children would burst into giggles and sing, *"Lale ki khopri par lai langar."*

In the meanwhile, Ahmed, Kallan, Shibbu and others were deeply absorbed in their game of *gutthi* and *unti*.

"Will you pass my *bunta?*"

"Why don't you aim the *paintra* from the rear?"

And this sequence of *bunta* and *paintra* went on all day. And several times a day a sharp, screeching voice would call out from the stairway opposite, and ring through the street from one end to the other.

"Ge—or—gie!"

"I'm just here, Ma," George would shout back.

Babu, startled, would look in the direction of the stairway and wink surreptitiously. Flora would flash a smile at him and disappear in the house.

Malik spent his day lolling on a charpoy in one corner as Malikin attended to him sitting closeby. Bose Babu's little daughter teased Lochan all the time, *"Loche, daal-bhat khoche, Loche."*

Oppressed by the heat emanating from his furnace, Deenu would sometime come wiping his nose on the edge of his *lungi* to sit under the Jamun tree. A shower of expletives would soon follow. A few children could be seen teasing the itenerant Chinese cloth merchant.

"*Chini mama choon-choon, chini mama choon-choon!*"

Bihari spent long hours perched on the highest boughs of the Jamun tree and singing film songs, his favourite being, "*Peena-pilana bhoola gayi, ek shahr ki laundiya.*"

By the evenings this cacophony would begin to tone down. Tired of playing all day, the children would go home. Shatranj and *chausar* grew less noisy before folding up. Amma began to tidy up her hawker's basket. The temple bells ringing intermitently created a ponderous atmosphere. A strange, nameless melancholy descended on the Jamun tree whose leaves began to look dull and listless.

The sturdy, outstretched branches of the Jamun tree rested on the two buildings like the protective arms of a father. The tree in whose lap innumerable children had been nurtured to grow into fine youngmen, and in whose shade the elderly found refuge from the trials and travails of life, was the axis of that entire neighbourhood.

That jamun tree stood steadfast between the two buildings like a watchful patriarch who keeps guard over his children waiting for the morning when they would come and play in its shade again.

1947 came and the *gora*, as in shatranj, got in a position where defeat was inevitable. However, it created a rift between Sohan Singh and Mirzaji. Communal riots broke out. The fire ignited at Sadar Bazaar and Paharganj, came down to Sabzi Mandi. The flag of Muslim League was hoisted on one, and the tricolour on the other branch of the Jamun tree, but they crashed against each other and landed on the ground along with the branches. The two arms of the patriarch were chopped off followed by his sons digging their nails into each other's breasts like maniacs. Blood squirted in streams and spattered across the father's face.

Killing and looting of each other's property started. Deenu's corpse was flung under the Jamun tree. One rioter said, "He is a Mussalman." Another said, "Let us burn him so that he goes straight to hell!" A third person started hacking the branches from the tree and flinging them on the dead body. A fourth tossed and piled his belongings on it. Suddenly a small tin container hit the chest of the corpse and a whole lot of marbles rolled out of it to lie scattered on the road.

Holding it by the leg, someone was about to throw Ahmed's body on the burning pyre but he stopped short. Others soon surrounded him.

"What has happened?"

"This is Nikka."

One said, "I say, burn him quickly so that Sohan Singh does not find out."

Residents of Fasih Building chopped off the branches from their side and set the bodies afire.

The corpses kept burning as the branches were hacked one after the other.

The *gora* was vanquished.

Now when I look at the Jamun tree my heart aches with a hollow feeling. The tree stands bereft and forlorn all the time.

What I now see is just a rough trunk with three or four

thick boughs and a few twisted branches with discoloured bark peeling off lore and there.

A large part of the tree on the side of Fasih Building has been hacked by the Municipal Committee in order to put up new electric cables. A solitary vendor selling *alu-chhole* sits under what remains of the tree and once in a way a charpoy stringer visits the street sending out a longish cry of "ch-ar-poy—bana—lo".

With its shade having been taken away from Jamun tree, there is nothing left. Nothing.

kagaz ki topi

When I was young, I looked more stupid than I actually was. Munni, however, was not only intelligent, she was also very beautiful. Everyone thought so. That is why, whenever the children of the neighbourhood playfully performed a marriage ceremony, Munni was always the bride — anyone could be bridegroom. The groom, his face veiled behind strings of flowers, would pretend to arrive on a horse. Sugar and *rotis* would be distributed to the marriage party. The groom would then lead the procession away singing, *"Main to Dilli se dulhan laya re ..."* The bride would walk behind him eating sugar by the handful.

Once, I pleaded with Munni, "Munni, let me be your bridegroom at least this time."

She looked at me scornfully, and said, "Go, look at your

face in the mirror!"

When I returned home that day, I gazed at my face in the mirror for a long time. I don't know why, but I was convinced that I wasn't handsome enough to be a bridegroom — that I looked like an idiot.

Munni was related to us. We used to play together. She would share her new toys with us, while I showed her the treasure I had accumulated — marbles with fantastic swirls, caps of soda-water bottles, pieces of coloured glass. She loved the colour red. I gave her all the pieces of red glass from my treasure trove. Then I spent days looking for more pieces of red glass for her. When I couldn't find any, I broke the red vase that stood on Babuji's table.

The next day, Munni and I fought for some reason and she threw away the pieces of red glass I had given her. I was very hurt. I took Kalloo aside and sitting on the steps poured out my tale of woe to him. I expected him to curse Munni and sympathise with me, but he only sat and wiped his running nose — I don't know if he even heard what I told him. No one ever said a word against Munni.

Even at home, my two brothers continued to play with Munni and ignored me. I sat alone and made toys out of old newspapers — sometimes a boat, sometime a cap and many airplanes. Those paper toys became a hit. The boys of the neighbourhood began to respect me. Even Munni agreed that in one of my large paper caps I could pass for a bridegroom. And I became a bridegroom.

One day, while I was painting something, Neeraj walked in. He glared at me. I was scared.

"Neeraj *bhaiya*, take this. I've made a kite for you."

Neeraj snatched the kite from my hand, tore it into shreds and ran away.

I began to tremble with rage. But I controlled myself because I knew that he was stronger than I was. He only had to twist my arm to break a bone. I was, after all, a weakling.

When Masterji came that evening to teach us, he dragged Neeraj into the house and asked, "Have you done those sums?"

"Yes," Neeraj replied, arrogantly.

"And the translation into English?"

"What? Oh, yes."

"Show me."

I was happy that he would finally get his just reward. But he suddenly picked up my copy-book and handed it over to Masterji. Before I could say anything, he twisted my arm so hard that I was afraid to say anything.

Time passed. Twenty years slipped by. I moved to Bombay. Munni's elder brother, Prakash, rented a large house at Juhu beach. I moved in with him, all the others went to Dehradun. Munni began to study there.

Two months ago, when Prakash got married, everyone came down to Bombay. Munni came too. Initially, she seemed rather grown up. But slowly, she once again became the girl I knew as a child, one full of zest and mischief. As long as she was formal, I was safe. But the moment she relaxed, she made my life difficult.

One day, I was sitting in my room writing something, when she walked in, pulled me out of my chair and took me outside. She pointed towards the beach, and said in a romantic voice, "Let's go for a long walk on the beach."

"Why?"

"To eat *chaat*."

She insisted on eating *chaat* every evening and on bathing in the sea every morning.

Once, when she was bathing in the sea, she suddenly slipped and went under. She came up spluttering. Water gushed out of her nose. Slightly embarassed, she regained her balance and walked back to the beach. She spat out the salty sea-water a few times. I imitated her. She took out all her anger at me.

That day, out of revenge, she added salt to my tea. When I mischievously gave my cup of tea to her mother, she snatched it out of her hand and ran away. Her mother was puzzled by what was going on and, to tell you the truth, so was I. I understood much later, after everything was over.

One afternoon, I was sitting at my desk and writing something when she looked in and said, "Hey Mister, what are you doing?" She had an ice-cream in her hand.

"Hey Mister?" Surprised, I looked at her.

"What are you writing?"

I smiled, but didn't reply.

"Didn't you hear what I said?" She screamed at me and threw her ice-cream on my papers. I jumped up in anger. But she had disappeared.

Sometimes, when she was in a good mood, she would come to my room and entertain me with anecdotes about her college or stories about her girl-friends.

"I have a girl-friend. A boy used to visit her everyday in the hostel. One day ..."

"Why did that boy visit your friend?"

"How should I know? The two of them ... I don't know," she would reply evasively.

"Why didn't you ask your girl-friend?"

Irritated, she would reply, "You always interrupt me when I tell you something." Then she would stomp out of the room. I, instead, would long for her to snatch the pen out of my hand, pick up my book, perch herself on my table, rest her chin on her hands and mock me, "Since you can't write, why do you ruin so many sheets of paper with black marks."

After sometime, a letter from Dehradun informed us that Neeraj was coming to Bombay. The moment Neeraj came, the house became lively. There was always laughter and song and fun. Life in the army had knocked out the little seriousness Neeraj had. He involved everyone in his stories and gossip. He turned the house upside-down. Neeraj thought of all sorts of new games and Munni always joined him. In fact, she began to spend her time happily with him. Slowly, she began to ignore my presence. I started spending most of my time away from the house.

One afternoon when I came home, I saw that Munni was wearing Neeraj's army uniform and had a cigarette in her hand. She was coughing badly because she had choked on the smoke. I turned around and left at once.

A few days later, she walked into my room and said, "Give back my photographs."

"I have pickled them," I said with a smile.

"Return them. What right have you to keep them?"

I got up and quietly handed them over to her.

"And the ones taken when I was bathing in the sea — where are they?"

"I don't know. I'll find them."

"I want them now."

"I don't have them with me."

In anger, she threw all the photographs on the table. I picked them up with both hands, tore them and threw them out of the window. She watched me in disbelief and then left without saying a word.

After that, we didn't talk to each other. Both of us were angry, and as Neeraj talked more than was necessary, no one noticed our silence.

Whenever I came back home in the evening, I would find her either playing cards with Neeraj in the verandah or absorbed in a game of carrom with her sister-in-law. She had also stopped eating *chaat*.

One night, I came home late. When I walked into my room, I found her sitting at my desk. Perhaps she had been reading the newspaper. As soon as she heard my footsteps, she got up and pretended to look for a book on the shelf. I had my back to her and was hanging up clothes in the almirah, when she said, "We are going back tomorrow."

"That's good news," I said. My words seem to bounce off the floor. She was hurt and stood in silence for a while. To tell you the truth, even I don't know why I was so harsh.

"Ammi was saying that ... we have to leave tomorrow."

I asked, "What would you like to do?"

She was quiet for some time. I looked towards her.

She had turned pale. In a tearful voice, she asked, "Are you still angry with me?"

It seemed to me as if she was going to break down and weep. But the moment I stepped forward to console her, she backed away towards the door. I thought she had something in her hand which she was trying to hide from me. I tried to grab her hand, but she slipped away leaving what she was holding. I saw that she had left behind a large paper cap.

junglenama

River Purna flows through the land where the jungles of terai end. By and large the river is placid, but often during the monsoons it grows turbulent and overflows its banks. Occasionally its waters erode the soil here and there and carry away the rocks and pebbles with them. On the other side of the river is a small hillock with a human settlement. At one time that area too was a jungle where animals like cheetahs, bears, monkeys, rats, mongooses and snakes used to live. Now all you see there are dogs who have become slaves to humans, or a few others who have given up the culture of the forest in order to be tamed and domesticated by man — cows, bulls, buffaloes and goats. As for the donkeys, they have always been asses anyway. But rumour has it that the big Chaudhary of the settlement keeps several horses and also an elephant named Mahabali. What is more, the horses are said to have been tamed into domestication by others of their own kind.

Of late the elders among the denizens of the jungle on this side of the river Purna had been feeling concerned about something grave. A mysterious terror seemed to be stalking the forest. You could see groups of animals talking in whispers to each other at different places. The fox and the jackal were whispering to each other at one place and half a dozen ostriches with their necks intertwined were deep in confabulation at another. They generally fell silent to see Cheetah coming in their direction. Every animal would sneak out to look beyond the jungle and across the river at the human settlement on some pretext or the other. The settlement was so populous that someone or the other was always seen working on the bank of the river on their side. For the last few days people in large numbers had been seen working in the river all day which had generated misgivings in the minds of the animals who were apprehensive that a bridge was coming up over the river.

At one time there was a jungle on the other side of the river Purna in which all the animals roamed trumpeting and roaring freely and leading a carefree life. God knows when and how a human settlement was established in the shadow of that hill. To begin with, the animals remained unconcerned about them. They thought that the humans had as much right over that land as animals themselves did. It is a fact that the land belonged to the animals in the beginning but when some of the species evolved to assume the shape and the culture of man, they accepted that every one had the right to live as they chose. Even today the animals demand that right. With the rapid pace of evolution men grew cleverer and that made them arrogant. The moment they learnt how to use weapons, they started believing that they were superior to others, and began to persecute animals. Their tyranny was put up with in the beginning but since everyone has a right to live, they started retaliating. Consequently, over a time, man moved out of the jungles to live in the plains and on the hills. They gave up the culture of the forest and started living in houses and settlements.

However, in spite of living in houses, villages and other settlements, man did not shed some of his beastly proclivities. He started enslaving the weaker among his own race. Over time his species was divided into different races, countries and religions. Different kinds of animals can still live together in a jungle but man does not even like to share a country with other men. He often divides a country. Families fight among themselves and houses get divided. He has no qualms about appropriating what rightfully belongs to others. What is more, man thrives on the misfortunes of those who are weaker than him. Such fears and misgivings had been floating in the air of the jungle for some days. All the animals could sense them but they were not able to arrive at a decision.

Finally an elder denizen spoke up in wrath, "These people have rendered us homeless a number of times. Ours is the last remaining jungle in the neighbourhood. Where shall we go if they construct a bridge and set up habitation here? At one time the entire earth belonged to us but now we are at the mercy of human beings for even a small patch of land. Their race does not become extinct. Now they are looking around for living space on the Moon and Mars. And then ....

"Oof! The human greed has really destroyed us!"

Another elder coughed as he shook his ears. He said, "These people have no shame at all. Just think it is only a few years since they have come and settled down under that hill. Then they proceeded to chop off our trees. Babbar Khan, the lion, had said right then that we should attack and kill a few of them. That would have chased them away. If they continue the way they are, we'd have to vacate this place some day." Babbar Khan was right. That is what is going to happen now.

Another added, "I still remember how swollen the river was when, perched on the shoulders of our aged parents, we had crossed over to this side under the cover of darkness."

"And those little ones who were swept away by the swift currents ... Only God knows what became of them."

"I still hear their shrieks," the elderly doe said, her eyes overbrimming with tears.

In addition to fear, an air of anxiety and desolation gradually pervaded the jungle air.

Suddenly the place was overtaken by a certain restlessness. It so happened that a youngster from the zebra family who had gone to the river to drink water was spotted by some people from the settlement on the other side and they started shouting. Thinking that a child from the settlement had fallen in the river and he could rescue him if he saw him, the zebra lifted his lead. Instantly some rocks landed on his back followed by an arrow that pierced his thigh. Turning around quickly, he ran back to the jungle. He could hear footsteps in the distance. The striped creature was hurrying homewards when he saw an innocent rabbit returning to his house falling prey to a bullet.

Babbar Khan the lion who had, for many days, been sitting inside his den and pondering over the whole situation, came down the mound around which a large number of animals were already gathered. They expressed their anguish pleadingly. The lion cleared his throat in acknowledgement of their angst and sat down against a rock.

A few birds flew in and perched on the branches of the trees nearby. Their destiny was bound to that of the quadrupeds. A long silence descended upon the assembly.

The mother of the slain rabbit sobbed hiding in a bush. The entire striped clan congregated in a close bunch at one place.

Cheetah came striding from one side and stood still. His eyes were burning a bright red. His entire family had been killed by the people from that settlement. He was the lone surviving member of his race.

Háthi Pershad, the elephant stroked Cheetah's back with his trunk, and through his eyes urged him to be patient.

Cheetah did not like it. He turned back and left the place without saying a word.

As the word spread, more and more animals arrived and congregated on the mound. Antelopes, wild boars and all. The slothful owl flew in too but closed his eyes and fell asleep instantly.

Suddenly Cheetah reappeared carrying the blood splattered body of a man. Everybody looked at him with disapproval for he seemed to have killed for revenge. But Cheetah said, "This man was killed and flung in the river by another man. I have carried him here to show you that those who have no pity for their own kind are not going to be concerned about us."

The lion's whiskers stood erect on their ends. He stood resolutely on his four legs and started speaking in a voice rising steadily. "We have already handed over in stages all the jungles on this land to the humans. We have compromised with their growing tribes and rising expectations. But man takes advantage of his racial superiority. He has invented all kinds of weapons with which he also kills his own kind. The man has turned into a beast. How can we expect those who have no pity for their own kind to have any consideration for us? For all I know, they may wipe us out from the earth. We are the original inhabitants of this land. They have already wiped out several species of animals but this time we are going to fight for the survival of our races."

All the animals cheered in affirmation of the lion's decision. The lion held his tail erect to direct them to stay quiet and continued, "But remember that we have to fight back unitedly if one of us is attacked irrespective of whether it is a cheetah or an ant."

All bent their knees and rubbed their snouts in the dust in acceptance. In the process an ostrich broke his back and started groaning with pain. A few animals burst out laughing but fell silent when Babbar Khan stood up again. The lion nominated a few leaders — an elephant, a bear, a fox and a horse and announced, "No one will act towards the protection of our forest without consulting this committee."

Cheetah was assigned the job of keeping an eye on the bridge the people from the settlement were constructing. All the monkeys were to assist him. Eagles were instructed to report any dubious activities taking place in the settlement.

Nothing happened for the next few days. People continued to work at the construction of the bridge which was gradually advancing towards the jungle.

One day a white eagle alighted on the mound and blew a long whistle. The lion came out. The eagle informed him, "A number of large cages have been brought to the settlement on the other side. Also there are guns in boxes which are locked up."

"Who has conveyed the news about the guns?"

"A cockroach told about them to a mouse and when the latter was about to run off with the news, a crow ...."

"A crow is a despicable bird," the lion interrupted, "he eats man's leftovers and filth."

"But he is extremely clever, *Raja*. He can cheat and deceive even man."

"The one who deceives is called cunning and not clever. Anyway, please continue with your report."

"All right. So the mouse told Kagaram the crow that he was going to the jungle with important news which concerns all the birds and animals. It is about their struggle for freedom. On hearing the news the crow carried him to the other side of the river and left him in the jungle where he still is and Kagaram is the one who has conveyed the news to me."

The lion cogitated for a while. Then he summoned the fox standing outside his den and instructed her to call a meeting of the committee.

The secret meeting of the committee went on all right.

The next day all the animals were assigned their duties and the war for the freedom of the jungle commenced.

The mice were instructed to infiltrate into all houses and collect information about guns and put a mark of identification where guns were stored.

"And how should we go about putting a mark on such houses, *Malik*?"

"Don't call anyone *malik*," the elephant scolded them. "This is something you have learnt from human beings. Physically we may be mightier than you are but that does not make us your master. You are a little shorter than we are but you know more tricks and that does not mean ...."

"Will you please talk of the relevant things, Hathi Pershad? You need to curb your tendency of talking too much."

The fox said jovially, "He does exaggerate everything. No wonder he has grown so huge!"

The horse stamped a hoof on the ground to silence the assembly, "Please stay quiet and talk only of the relevant things."

Turning to the mouse, Hathi Pershad asked, "What was your question, Chuhe Lal?"

"How should we go about putting a mark on the houses?"

The bear offered a suggestion, "How about telling the mice to nibble at and destroy the cartridges wherever they find them?"

The assembly accepted the idea and thus the mice made their first attack.

For two days no news was received in the jungle. Everybody wondered as to what had happened.

On the third day the monkeys brought the information that countless dead mice were being thrown into the streets in the settlement.

"It seems the cartridges had been laced with some poison which has killed the mice."

A pall of gloom hung over the colony of the mice

At night the lion offered his condolences to the small creatures. He said, "It was a mouse who nibbled at a net to set me free one day. I'm still indebted to the mice for saving my life. Please do not lose heart. Be bold and courageous. Right now we are fighting a mighty war in which your parents have laid their lives."

On hearing these words, instead of shedding tears, Cheetah's eyes blazed red with anger and he walked away from that place.

The complete update on the guns and ammunition was still eluding the animals. The dead mice had been flung out of innumerable houses. How was one to know where the cartridges were stored?

The bear came up with an old-fashioned idea. "Let us leave a beautiful doe to roam the streets of the settlement. Someone or the other is bound to come out of his house with a gun on seeing her. We'll then know that there are guns in that house."

The elephant objected vehemently to this suggestion. "You mean to say you would have the hapless doe killed?"

"Please let me finish," said the bear. "We'll have the crows perch on the roofs and parapets of the houses. The moment someone takes out the gun, they would warn her by shouting 'run-run'. She would then escape and the house would be identified."

"But what makes you think that the crows would act at our behest?"

"Why shouldn't they? After all their original culture is the culture of the jungles."

"But how does one approach them?"

"This Kagaram has been staying in the jungle for some days. I had been told about him by Ullu Mian, the owl."

"I'm sure Ullu Mian just dreamt of him! Doesn't he sleep all the time?"

"Please don't say that. He is an extremely wise elder who keeps an eye on everything."

"But I'd like to suggest one thing. Please don't tell the lion about this scheme. He hates crows."

"We'll go about it on our own. I'm sure the King would be happy the day we convey the information about cartridges to him."

They approached the herd of the antelopes and told them about their scheme. The deers were frightened at the idea but Sunaini the doe came forward.

"I am willing. I know I can perform this duty."

A number of deers held their breath at her courage and tried to prevent her from going. "No, no, Sunaini. Think of your eighteen-month old baby."

"So what? It's a boy and not a girl," answered Sunaini. She was prepared to go.

Kagaram flew up to the settlement and confabulated with the local crows. They agreed to make a noise but none of them were prepared to risk their lives.

"Where is the risk to your life in this? All we have to do is sit on the roofs, parapets and electric cables. The moment we see someone with a gun, we would start shouting, 'run-run'."

The next morning Sunaini started moving around leaping and prancing in the streets of the settlement. The crows took positions to keep a watch over houses and waited for someone with a gun to come out so that they could start shouting 'run-run'.

A number of people tried to capture Sunaini by offering her food but she was not to be lured by such temptations. Some of them then approached the Chaudhary.

"A very beautiful doe is freely and fearlessly roaming our streets. Please come out for *shikar* and shoot her."

The moment the Chaudhary stepped out of his *haveli* holding a walking stick, the excited crows started shouting 'run-run' and flew in the direction of the doe who was quite far from there. Hearing the commotion she sprinted towards the river but some people threw a net on her and captured her alive.

After a while the Chaudhary arrived at the spot on horse-back. He paid some money to the captors and bought the doe from them. Tying a rope around her neck, he made her follow his horse to the *haveli*.

Returning to the jungle, Kagaram narrated the whole episode to the others.

The lion was outraged, "Who sent Sunaini to the settlement?"

The faces of all the members of the committee fell. They confessed their guilt. The lion roared again, "And you left her under the care of those wretched crows who don't know a gun from a walking stick!"

He paced up and down in a fury. At length he came out with a suggestion, "In my opinion the guns and ammunition are kept in the Chaudhary's house. He seems to be the greatest man of the settlement."

Everyone agreed with him readily. "Yes, yes. We also think so."

But the owl who was perched on the branch of a tree yawned long and slow and opened his eyes, "He is the richest man of the settlement, not the greatest."

"Then who is the greatest?"

"The Police Station Officer. The place is governed according to the wishes of the Chaudhary but the orders are passed by the *thanedaar*."

"We have information that some large cages have been brought to the settlement and also boxes of guns and ammunition. Could you tell us where they are most likely to be stored?

"In the police station. Where else would the *thanedaar* store them?"

All of them looked at each other. The lion roared, "That is the most dangerous place because it is guarded even at night."

The fox had a brainwave. She said, "The guard is kept in the front whereas the stuff must be stored in the godown at the rear of the building. If only we could open its door!"

Ullu Mian interjected, "Don't be ridiculous, Lomrhi Bi. Will you open the door with a key? You should say 'If only we could break open that door.' "

The elephant volunteered to do the needful. "I'll break open that door. If we can break the doors of the forts for man, can't we pull down the door of a godown for our own sake?"

Babbar Khan the lion cautioned him, "You are not exactly an insect who could escape unspied. What if you are caught?"

"But I will go at night."

"It is not done," thundered the lion.

The fox asked again, "So how shall we open the door of the godown?"

The lion took a deep breath and said, "Cheenti Rani the ant would have the door of the godown broken."

"How would she?" Everyone stared incredulous at the lion.

Cheenti Rani was sent for. She arrived accompanied by five handmaidens. The lion explained the entire scheme to her. "Rani, please go with your finest battalion and overpower Mahabali, the Chaudhary's elephant. He would trumpet and scream but you make your way to his flappers and tell him that he should accompany you to the godown and smash it's door otherwise you'll enter his ear and kill him. I am sure he will oblige."

All the animals stared in open-mouthed astonishment.

"What a clever strategy! If it is inevitable that someone should die, let it be a traitor!"

"We do not want any animal to be slain." The lion explained the rest of the plan in detail. "As the elephant approaches the door, five hundred bats shall swoop down over the constables outside the police station so that they rush indoors for cover. Shut all doors and windows. In this way the noise of the door being broken would not reach them."

"After the door is broken one and a half thousand fireflies would enter the godown and light up the place. The elephant would trample over and destroy the cases containing guns and ammunition. This operation would be carried out by night and all of us would come back before dawn."

All of them cheered in loud unison.

Everything was followed according to the plans. They overpowered Mahabali and made him leave the *haveli* without a sound. The bats descended on the police station on the cue, swooped down on the constables and confounded them. The fireflies illumined the godown to the brightness of the day. The guns and the ammunition were crushed down and destroyed. However, it was morning by the time the mission was accomplished and when a worn-out Mahabali was emerging from the godown, he was seen by the *thanedaar*.

The *thanedaar* rushed to the godown and surveyed the scene. He turned on his heels and ran after the elephant. Staggering with fatigue, the elephant had streaks of perspiration on his brow. The *thanedaar* thought the elephant had run amok and he would definitely go on a rampage in the settlement. So he promptly took out his pistol and pumped all five bullets into the elephant's head.

Mahabali gave out a long trumpet cry after which he collapsed on the ground, writhed in pain for a while and died.

The jungle elephant Hathi Pershad had tears in his eyes when this news reached him. Mahabali was the son of his elder paternal aunt.

The next day the jungle was pervaded by a calm which was marked more by courage and less by fear. The animals had won their initial move but nobody knew how the people from the settlement would retaliate. Work was progressing steadily on the bridge and it was obvious that it would be completed in a few days.

Stationed on the mound of earth, the members of the committee waited for the news all day. The white eagle flew back and forth several times and there was no sign of Kagaram's call for miles.

Evening gradually gave way to the night.

The next day and night were also spent in the same manner. The bridge on the river was now extended almost to the bank on the side of the jungle.

Cheetah continued to keep a vigil through the nights. One night he heard someone crying. He went to investigate only to find a fawn hiding in the bushes closeby.

"Who are you, son, and what are you doing here?" Cheetah asked.

"I am Sunaini's son. My mother has been captured on the other side of the river. I want to go to her. Ullu Mian has told me that she is at the Chaudhary's house. I'll ask the Chaudhary to keep me and release my mother. Please take me there."

Cheetah felt sorry for Sunaini's son.

"Look, child, the Chaudhary will keep you but he won't set your mother free."

"I won't mind that. I'll at least be there to take care of my mother."

"It won't be like that. He'll sell you to the zoo. And what if he sells the two of you to different places?"

Suchal the fawn fell silent but tears continued to pour out of his eyes. After a moment's silence Cheetah asked again, "Why didn't you approach the lion? After all your mother had gone to the settlement for the sake of the denizens of his kingdom."

Suchal bowed his head and said slowly, "I didn't have the courage to go to the king."

"Come along with me." And Cheetah took Sunaini's son to the lion.

The fox was sitting outside the den on guard duty. She said the king was resting after a long meeting with the white ants.

"White ants? Who are they?"

"You live in the jungle and don't know who the white ants are? The white ants can devour the entire jungle in a night if they want. They can eat up iron, rocks wood and all."

"But what did the lion expect from them?"

Hearing their voices the lion came out of his den and asked, "What is the matter? How come you are here and not keeping an eye on the bridge?"

As it was, Cheetah was quite short-tempered. He got irritated and answered, "What is the use of keeping a watch over that bridge? It is going to be completed tomorrow."

"Not completed but destroyed. I have just ordered the white ants to see to it that hollow fragments of the bridge are seen floating in the river by tomorrow. It is going to be a crucial night. Please go back and keep a vigil at your post. Let us know if anybody tries to infiltrate to this side.

"You have no idea how faithfully the herds of elephants, packs of wolves, families of bats, bears and foxes stay awake through the nights to keep a watch over things. They are willing to lay down their lives on just one call from me." After this exhortation the lion went back to his den.

Cheetah returned to the bridge feeling both surprised and perplexed. Suchal was following him sobbing quietly. Suddenly Cheetah turned to him and taking his hand, said,

"Come, let's go to other side of the bridge. We'll bring back Sunaini before the bridge is demolished."

He had made up his mind on the spur of the moment. He arrived in the settlement with Suchal in a short while.

They pussy-footed their way through the deserted streets till they reached the Chaudhary's *haveli*. But how were they to find out where Sunaini was kept in such a huge building?

They noticed a cat scaling a wall. In an instant Cheetah had pulled her down by the tail. The cat was petrified. Cheetah boxed her ears and warned her, "If you make a noise, I'll wipe out your entire race. Tell me quickly where the Chaudhary has tethered Sunaini the doe?"

"In a small room behind the stable. That is where she is imprisoned."

"How does one reach that room?" Cheetah asked.

"Follow me. I'll take you there," the cat answered.

On reaching the room they found a heavy lock hanging on its door. The window was bolted from inside. There was only one way of getting inside and that was through the ventilator at the top. Cheetah said to the cat, "Jump in through the ventilator and open the window. I'll take care of the rest."

The cat followed his instructions. As soon as the window was opened, he went inside, snapped the rope and brought Sunaini out. Sunaini went crazy with joy on seeing Suchal. She began to kiss and caress him but Cheetah warned her, "Hurry up and flee the settlement fast otherwise we'll be caught."

The cat wanted to leave. She said, "Meow?"

Cheetah allowed her to go with a warning, "No one should

know of what has happened here tonight."

The cat promised not to tell anybody and left. But she turned traitor and bounced into the Chaudhary's bedroom where she deliberately toppled a flower vase to wake him up. When he got up she went and stood in the balcony so that he would follow her.

Cheetah, Sunaini and Suchal happened to be passing through the street at that moment. They were walking close to the walls so that nobody could spy them from the balconies. But when Cheetah lifted his eyes in response to the cat's "meow" he saw the Chaudhary standing and stretching his limbs on the balcony.

His blood began to boil at the sight. It took him no time to recognize the man who had murdered his parents, had their bodies skinned and sold the hides to an Englishman. His mind began to reel with the thoughts of revenge. He turned to Sunaini and Suchal, "Run as fast as you can, cross the bridge and reach the jungle. I'll follow you in a while."

"But where are you going?"

"Don't ask questions and do as I tell you."

After sending off Sunaini and Suchal, Cheetah looked up at the balcony again. His eyes blazed with red hot anger. He scaled the wall noiselessly, leapt up to a tree and from there jumped down on the balcony. The Chaudhary had already gone back to bed by then.

Suddenly opening his eyes, he caught sight of the glowing ambers of Cheetah's eyes and let out a mighty scream. Cheetah pounced upon him and finished him off in one blow.

Sunaini and Suchal reached the other end of the bridge and started waiting for Cheetah. They started getting anxious when he did not return till morning. Alarmed, they decided to meet the lion and apprise him of all that had happened the previous night.

The lion was flabbergasted at the news. "What a shocking thing to have happened! How could Cheetah make such a terrible mistake? I have always been afraid his bad temper would be his undoing."

He paced up and down for long.

Then he sent off the white eagle on an urgent mission. "Please go and get us news about where Cheetah is and how he is doing."

The news spread all over like wild fire. All the birds and animals were anxious. Cheetah was the last remaining specimen of his race. He was the glory of the jungle. An ominous calm pervaded the air in the jungle once again.

The white eagle returned and gave the news, "The Chaudhary has been killed and Cheetah has been captured. He is badly injured. He is going to be put into a large cage and sent to the city zoo today. A swift horse-drawn carriage is being readied for that purpose."

The fox proposed that they should call an urgent meeting and arrange for the release of Cheetah by hook or by crook.

The lion snorted angrily and dismissed the proposal.

"Then what do you propose to do?"

"I'll go personally to rescue him. This is not the time for discussion. This is the time for action."

The lion marched towards the bridge right away.

As he reached the bridge he noticed that it was disintegrating and falling down in chunks. The white ants had accomplished their mission. However, the lion was not deterred even for a moment. He jumped into the river to the astonishment of the other denizens of the jungle.

The appearance of the lion in the settlement on the other side of the river caused a stampede. People ran for cover to their houses. The white eagle flew overhead blowing long whistling calls to guide the lion through the streets.

A horse carriage was parked in readiness outside the police station. The iron cage with the imprisoned Cheetah had already been placed atop the carriage. A large crowd had gathered to see Cheetah.

The crowd disintegrated and people ran helter-skelter on hearing the roar of the lion. Terrified, the horses bolted and galloped away in panic. The lion gave chase.

Wreaking havoc with property in the lanes and streets, the horses made their way to the road running parallel to the river till they reached a turn where the lion blocked their way. As the lion sprang on them, one of the horses fell in a swoon and the other scampered away on three legs. The lion chewed at the iron bars, broke the cage and Cheetah was set free.

However, Cheetah was in a semiconscious state at that time. The lion placed him around his shoulders and jumped into the river. Other animals were already waiting on the bank when they reached there. All of them proclaimed in unison, "The king of the jungle is the real king!"

Cheetah's condition was deteriorating. Ullu Mian devised and tried a lot of remedies but none of them worked. In spite of all efforts, Cheetah breathed his last after three days.

The next day some people from the settlement came to the other side of the river in a boat. An old man named Salim Ali who loved birds was among them. They were carrying a long signboard with them.

They left in a few hours time after installing the signboard in the jungle. The board had the following legend —

WILDLIFE IS AS PRECIOUS AS HUMAN LIFE.

IT IS OUR DUTY TO PRESERVE IT.

(NATIONAL WILDLIFE SANCTUARY)

glossary

adda: hiding/meeting place
alu: potato
Ameen: so be it
amrit: nectar
angeethi: an earthenware heating device with live coal
Arrey: a form of addressing "Hey"
bada: big
Badshah (salamat): Emperor (long live)
baithak: sitting/meeting area
bajri: maize
betay: daughter
Bhagyawan: My Lord
bhajan: holy songs sung in praise of the almighty
bhaijan: brother dear

bidi: country cigarette
bunta: marble
chaat: a sweet and sour savoury
chacha: father's younger brother
chaupal: main meeting ground in villages
chausar: a game of dice
choli: blouse
chor: thief
chulha: cooking stove
cowries: traditional dice
dal: pulses
dharma: one's religion
dhoti: Long cloth tied at the waist and wrapped around the
    legs.
dhurrie: mat
dhut-tere-ki: Curse be to you/An expression of "Oh! Hell!"
fasal: crop
ghazals: couplets put to music
ghee: clarified butter
ghia-ghas: a grater
gilli-danda: a traditional game played by children with a long
    stick and an oblong shaped object.
gora: white
granthi: priest of the Sikh community
Hai! hai: a lamentation
hakim: doctors using natural elements for curing ailments
halal: the method of slaughtering goats — Muslim style
Har har Mahadev: Glory to Lord Shiva
hijrat: pilgrimage
Hindustan Zindabad: Long live India
hookah: a traditional smoking pipe

hukum: My lord
huzoor: sir
Inshallah: God willing
Jai Ramji: Praise to Lord Ram
Jamun: blackberry
Jhoola: swing
Jo bole so nihal/sat siri akal: Blessed be those who hail thy
    name
kaka: a term of endearment, usually to the youngest
khes: a warm covering used during the winter months
kholi: a one-room tenement usually in the slum area
kos: about 3 miles
langar: a free meal usually at holy places
lassi: buttermilk
lungi: a loose sarong-like dress
Main to Dilli se dulhan laya re: I have brought a bride from Delhi
malik: owner
malkin: owner (feminine)
mamaji: mother's brother
mandap: place where marriage ceremony takes place
manjha: thread used to fly kites
mantra: holy incantations
miyan: Mister
mukhiya: head of the village
murdabad: curse be to you
naga: serpent
namkin: salty
nana: grandfather
nanak naam jahaz hai/jo chade so utare par: Guru Nanak has
    a thousand names/he who believes will reach the other
    shore

nani: grandmother
nullah: ditch
paan: betel leaf
pallu: the part of the saree draped over the shoulder
parandi: an ornamental braid
parantha: a thick chapati with stuffings
peena pilana bhoola gaye/ek shahar ki laundiya: He has even
    forgotten to drink because of the city-girl
pucca: solid
puja: offerings to the Gods
purohit: temple priest
qasbah: moffussil town
Raja: King
roti: chapati
Saala: bloody
sadhu: ascetic
Sankranti: the first day of the Hindu month
sangam: confluence
sapt rishis: seven stars
Sardar: Chief
shamshan: cremation ground
shikar: hunt
Stapu: a variation of hopscotch
tandoor: an earthen oven
thanedaar: term for the police of the village districts
tilak: a vermillion mark on the forehead
ustad: teacher
waheguru: Praise to the Lord
zenana: women's quarters